PATTERN OF PEOPLE

By Elizabeth Goudge

ISLAND MAGIC

A CITY OF BELLS

A PEDLAR'S PACK

TOWERS IN THE MIST

THE MIDDLE WINDOW

THE SISTER OF THE ANGELS

THE BIRD IN THE TREE

SMOKY HOUSE

THE GOLDEN SKYLARK

THE WELL OF THE STAR

THE HEART OF THE FAMILY

THE BLUE HILLS

THE CASTLE ON THE HILL

GREEN DOLPHIN STREET

THE ELIZABETH GOUDGE READER

THE LITTLE WHITE HORSE

SONGS AND VERSES

PILGRIM'S INN

GENTIAN HILL

THE REWARD OF FAITH

GOD SO LOVED THE WORLD

THE VALLEY OF SONG

THE ROSEMARY TREE

THE WHITE WITCH

MY GOD AND MY ALL

THE DEAN'S WATCH

THE SCENT OF WATER

A BOOK OF COMFORT

A DIARY OF PRAYER

A CHRISTMAS BOOK

A BOOK OF PEACE

THE TEN GIFTS

THE CHILD FROM THE SEA

THE LOST ANGEL

THE JOY OF THE SNOW

A BOOK OF FAITH

PATTERN OF PEOPLE

Pattern of People

An ELIZABETH GOUDGE Anthology

arranged by Muriel Grainger

Coward, McCann & Geoghegan, Inc.
New York

First American Edition 1979
Copyright © 1976 by Muriel Grainger.
First printed 1978.

Library of Congress Cataloguing in Publication Data

Goudge, Elizabeth,
    Pattern of people.
    I. Grainger, Muriel.   II. Title.
    PZ3.G717Pat   1979   [PR6013.074]   823'.9'12   78-12123
    ISBN   0-698-10965-1

Printed in Great Britain by
Lowe & Brydone Printers Limited, Thetford, Norfolk

Contents

Foreword

OPEN ANY BOOK BY ELIZABETH GOUDGE, and you are immediately
in the company of unforgettable characters—lovable, fascinating,
sometimes eccentric, occasionally wayward—but real people
whose lives are woven together into the most enchanting patterns.

Here, in this selection from her work, the best of her portraits
are to be found—portraits of men and women, and delightful
miniatures of children, in which she excels. Some seem sketched in
pastels, living as they do in the world of yesterday, and they bring
with them a nostalgia for a time that is past; some move within
periods that are long ago and far away. Miss Goudge's most loved
creations are etched indelibly on the minds of those who have once
met them—characters like old Isaac, the watch-mender, or the du
Frocq family on "the Island", who appear here in two complete
tales.

In this collection, not only have some of her best short stories
been gathered together, but tales-within-a-tale are included too,
adapted from her novels with only the very minor alterations
involved in presenting them as stories in themselves. These may
serve as introductions to the books from which they are taken to
those who do not yet know them, and as a happy reminder of past
pleasure to those who do. A short extract from Miss Goudge's
autobiography, *The Joy of the Snow*, also appears here, for it too is a
story in its own right.

So here is a pattern of people—a pattern woven in true colours
with an extra strand of gold that is Elizabeth Goudge's unique
contribution. It shines through all her work, and arouses an
immediate response in those who meet and fall in love with the
people in her pages.

MURIEL GRAINGER

Woven From the Past

Lucy in London

IT WAS A PERFECT day in June, 1640, and the scent of the first wild roses came to the lowered coach window as Mrs. Gwinne drove with her ten-year-old grand-daughter Lucy through the meadows surrounding the village of St. Giles, and left them only as the coach bumped over the cobbles of Drury Lane. The lane was lined with houses now and Mrs. Gwinne deplored it. The pace at which London was spreading was causing a good deal of anxiety at this time. The walled city of London and the city of Westminster were now the body of a growing octopus, with tentacles reaching out to the villages of Stepney, Wapping and Kensington, and even to the fishing village of Putney, and not all the proclamations of King James and King Charles against new buildings had been able to halt the growth. "These foreigners who are here now are to blame for the over-crowding," lamented Mrs. Gwinne. "The new industries bring them, and of course the sea port and the new docks. They must live somewhere, poor things, one understands that, but where will it all end? How ugly these new houses are! Drury Lane was charming in the old days."

They drove on to London Wall and passed through the great gate into the old city that had always been here. The streets were very narrow and the traffic dense, carts and coaches jostling each other with great noise and confusion, for these streets had been made for men on horseback and for street barrows, not for the modern wheeled traffic.

At Paul's Cross they got out of the coach, and the old coachman was told to do some errands for Mrs. Gwinne and to fetch them later. Then they walked up the steps to the Cathedral. It was in a bad way just now for the spire had fallen and not been rebuilt, and much of the nave was in a ruinous state, but it was still a fine building. It surprised Lucy to find ladies and gentlemen using the nave as they used the piazza at Covent Garden, as a place for walking about together, and laughing and talking. There were plenty of children there too, playing games in corners, and one or two dog fights were in progress and no sexton came with the tongs to remove the fighters.

"It is not noisy like this in St. David's Cathedral," Lucy said to her grandmother.

"St. David's Cathedral is in Wales," replied Mrs. Gwinne. She needed to say no more. She and her grandchild, two exiles from a better country who lived their lives upon a higher plane, withdrew from the crowd and paced together down a quiet aisle, a place where sunlight touched the tombs of the dead, and their memorials upon the wall were silvery with the same soft dust that had drifted like sand into unswept corners, and like sand took the imprint as they passed of the slender feet of the lady and the child. Behind them the distant sound of the people was a sea surge. In front of them the sea caves of the holy places held only echo. . . .

There was a sound of mingled pattering and piping, as though a lot of small birds were singing through a spring shower beating on broad leaves. They looked round and saw a crocodile of little boys walking briskly up the nave two by two, weaving in and out of the promenade of ladies and gentlemen as expertly as a lizard through grass. They had bright shining faces, and their piping voices, as they chattered together, were sharp and clear. Black gowns lifted back from their shoulders and their thick shoes on the worn paving stones went clackety-clack with a heartening cheerfulness. They disappeared into the shadows and the sound of rain and birdsong died away.

"The choristers of St. Paul's," said Mrs. Gwinne. "When we see them again they will have their surplices on and the service will begin."

Already the organ was playing and quietness was falling upon the nave. Some of the ladies and gentlemen were going away and others were finding seats and talking to each other only quietly. Two men in black gowns, whom Lucy took to be a sexton and beadle such as they had had at home in Wales, were shooing out children and dogs. Mrs. Gwinne and Lucy found seats in the nave and sat down and waited.

Presently they saw the little boys again, coming out of the shadows and filing up to the choir two by two, silent and decorous. The gentlemen singers and the cathedral dignitaries followed them and the service began.

Lucy had never heard music like this. It rose and fell, sometimes a mere thread of sound, sometimes a swell of glory. Now and then the music ceased altogether and a voice could be heard reading from the word of God, or praying. No words could be distinguished from where they sat, but the voice had a strange far-off beauty as though someone was speaking of glory from beyond the confines of the world. . . .

After the final blessing, Mrs. Gwinne took her grandchild by the hand and led her firmly from the building.

. . ."Now for the bridge," Lucy said joyously, and leaving her grandmother she ran on ahead to find the coach.

The southern boundary of the city was the river and they drove through the south gate on to London Bridge itself. Though there were thirty landing places on the Thames there was only this one bridge, and to Lucy it seemed one of the glories of the world. Eighteen great arches carried the famous shopping centre right across the river. The buildings were tall and some of the houses above the shops were carried by arches across the street. Between the blocks of buildings there were open bays and here one could lean over the wall and see the river and watch the shipping. The shops on the bridge held everything the heart could desire, silks and velvets, jewels and silverware, perfumes and spices from the East, fine china and delicate glassware. Everything that the ships brought up the river found its way to London Bridge. There was even a shop that sold parrots and lapdogs, and little monkeys and marmosets such as the Queen loved. Being so small herself Henrietta Maria liked diminutive creatures and people said that when she travelled she was followed by a whole coach full of monkeys and dwarfs. Lucy had visited this shop once before but it had broken her heart to see these little creatures. Their eyes were so sad as they sat shivering in their cages. There had been one especially, silver in colour with a black face, who had looked at her as though imploring her to buy him. But she had had no money then, and Mrs. Gwinne had told her this morning that a marmoset would cost more than one silver piece. Yet she could not forget him. "If we go past the shop today," she told herself, "I will shut my eyes."

They moved slowly along the bridge, stopping here and there for Mrs. Gwinne to make a few purchases. She was not a wealthy woman, least of all now with her grandchildren needing so much help, and she bought only a few things and these only after careful consideration. Lucy was not bored for everything she saw fascinated her, and today, for the first time in her life, she had money to spend. If her silver piece would not buy a marmoset it might buy the red shoes she saw in the window of the third shop they entered. She had always wanted red shoes. While Mrs. Gwinne was rubbing a piece of green cloth between finger and thumb, testing its worthiness to be made into a winter cloak and hood for her granddaughter, Lucy ran out of the shop to look at the shoes from outside. Running away from her grandmother was the last thing she intended, and she would have been back beside her again in a moment had it not been for the sudden excitement that broke out on the bridge.

"The Prince! The Prince! Coming up the river!" First one voice cried it out and then another, and there was a stampede of the passers-by to the open bays between the shops upon the east side of the bridge. There was one not far from the shop and Lucy was off like the wind. She would get to the front against the parapet or she would die. Diving this way and that wherever she saw an opening, thrusting with her sharp elbows and kicking hard, with her pink hood lost and her rose-coloured gown torn, she reached the parapet. But she could not get to the front for a solid line of bodies was leaning over it. Almost weeping with frustration she attacked the three backs nearest to her; slim backs clad in well-cut doublets, emerald green, silver grey and periwinkle blue. The emerald back had a familiar look and upon that she beat the hardest; then as its owner swung round with an oath she wriggled in between him and the taller figure in blue and hooked herself over the parapet of the bridge, clinging like a limpet with hands and feet and the whole of her defiant body. Let them unhook her if they dare!

"Lucy, you little devil!" ejaculated her brother's friend, Tom Howard. He began to explain who she was and they all three burst out laughing, and the young man in blue put his arm round her to protect her from the pressure of the crowd behind them. She glanced up briefly, smiling, then turned back towards the river, for the barge was coming towards them.

He was coming up the river to Whitehall. The busy traffic on the water had come to a standstill, the boats and barges drawing in to the banks with the men pulling off their hats and cheering and the women waving their handkerchiefs. Were the King and Queen there? asked the gossips on the bridge. No, only Prince Charles and the Earl of Newcastle, his tutor, and his gentlemen, said a man behind Lucy. They wouldn't be cheering like that if the King and Queen were there. But everyone loved the Prince. Even the Puritans. It was said the Puritans wanted to depose the King and put the Prince on the throne. "Traitor devils!" murmured Tom Howard hotly, but the young man in blue who held Lucy replied under his breath, "It might be the answer."

Then Lucy heard no more for the barge was coming nearer and the people on the bridge were beginning to cheer too. The golden summer day was turning towards evening and a cool breeze came over the water, lifting the folds of the Royal Standard flying from the stern of the barge. It came strongly forward, two white-crested waves rippling back from the prow, the banks of oars rising and falling in perfect time. The level sunlight gleamed on the flashing blades of the oars and glinted back in points of light from the gilded carving of the barge. All was a swift movement of colour and light held in the blue of water and sky like a gliding star, the mysterious planet that had shone when the Prince was born.

He stood bareheaded in the prow, waving his hat to the cheering people. He was a tall boy for his age and stood very erect, with dignity and grace. His hair fell to his shoulders, black and shining. His doublet was of golden satin with a big white lace collar that contrasted startlingly with the darkness of his skin. The barge had come almost to the bridge and he looked up at the cheering people crowded against the balustrade, lifting his hat and smiling at them in the way he had been taught, but holding the smile with difficulty, licking his lips now and then when they grew stiff and dry with the effort. Lucy saw his face more clearly than she had ever seen anything in her life, a square face dominated by the big nose and the large dark eyes. The Prince, looking up, saw the little girl leaning over the parapet and knew with the instinct that all children have that here was someone of his own age. His difficult smile changed to a grin so merry and infectious that Lucy's intentness broke up and with the whole of her self she smiled back at him, her eyes sparkling. He tipped his head far back and they laughed and waved to each other until the last second. Then the barge shot forward under the bridge and he was gone.

She was so tired, she found, that when the young man in blue lifted her down from the wall she could scarcely stand and was glad to hold to his sleeve.

"You have lost your hood, Lucy," said Tom Howard. "And torn your gown. What a gipsy you are."

"Has she run away from her mother?" asked the other young man. Lucy, coming to herself again, looked up into the face above the blue sleeve to which she was clinging. She considered both the strange young men, flashing her glance from one to the other so piercingly that they laughed. They were brothers, she thought, for they were alike, tall and good to look at, with the easy manner of those who have never made contact with the necessity for earning a living. . . .

Tom told her their names, Algernon and Robert Sidney. It was Algernon who was dressed in dove grey and Robert who wore periwinkle blue. Though she had not heard their illustrious name before Lucy sensed that these were young men upon whom the Princess from whom she believed she was descended would have looked with a favourable eye, and she walked away between them with an air of such delicate yet comical dignity that they laughed again. Then her mood changed, as she suddenly became aware of grave financial loss. "My silver piece!" she cried, and pulling her hand from Algernon's she ran back towards the river wall, thrusting the people aside that she might search among the cobbles for her lost treasure. Tom Howard blushed for shame, disassociating himself from this dishevelled little bantam hen scrabbling for corn, but both the Sidneys followed her and endeavoured to be helpful.

"It was a large silver piece?" asked Algernon.

Lucy lifted a flushed face. "It was not large but Doctor Cosin gave it to me. When the Prince came I must have dropped it."

"We will not find it now," said Robert gently. "Do not grieve, Lucy. I will give you another silver piece. What do you long for? A marmoset?"

Lucy looked up at him, as transfigured as though she had lifted the edge of a curtain and looked into heaven. Then the curtain dropped again. "No," she said. "A pair of shoes. A silver piece would not buy a marmoset."

"But you want a marmoset," said Robert. "And I have several silver pieces and I want to give you a marmoset. Shall we choose one?"

The words were hardly out of his mouth before she was running across the bridge, in and out of the traffic, making for the pet shop upon the other side. Horrified, he leaped after her, afraid she would be run over. Laughing, Algernon returned to Tom.

Lucy's face was pressed against the shop window when Robert caught up with her, her eyes searching anxiously among the little creatures within. "There was a special one," she said, in desperate anxiety lest it should be gone. "Silver and small. There it is."

"That one in the corner?" he asked dubiously, for the poor little creature looked very fragile. But Lucy was no longer with him. She was in the shop and had the marmoset in her arms. He followed her and looked into the great dark eyes so tragically set in a tiny velvet mask of a face. The eyes were too sorrowful to reflect light, and the silver body had become tarnished with misery, but the promise of beauty was there in the whiskers that fringed the little face; they shone in the sun like threads of fine spun glass. And it knew how to cling to what it wanted. It had its forearms round Lucy's neck, its tail was endeavouring to encircle her waist and it was giving little frantic cries of pleading. Lucy too knew what she wanted. Her eyes pierced straight through the doubtful Robert, transfixing him to her will.

Nevertheless he made enquiries of the salesman as to the marmoset's age and health. It was a young one, he was told, and valuable, but it had been difficult to keep alive because its mother had died; but with a good home it should not now be difficult to rear. With his back to Lucy Robert took out his purse and paid for the creature. When he turned to her again she was holding the marmoset in the crook of one arm as she had seen so many mothers holding an ailing child, and her face was grave. The child who had rushed across the road to find the marmoset had vanished now in someone much older. "I believe he cost too much," she said in a low voice. "But I cannot give him back for if I do not have him he will die. Can you afford it?"

He respected her feelings, and he did not laugh as he assured her that he could afford the marmoset.

"Thank you," said Lucy. "Thank you for my marmoset. His name is Jacob."

They crossed the bridge again and found Algernon Sidney and Tom with a very shaken Mrs. Gwinne. The face that she turned on her granddaughter was sterner than Lucy had ever seen it. "Madam, I did not mean to run away," she said.

Mrs. Gwinne, believing her, gravely inclined her head and by intuitive mutual consent the thrashing out of this matter was postponed until later. But the stern glance was not relaxed. It passed on to the marmoset and remained there.

"His name is Jacob," said Lucy with rock-like firmness.

Robert explained, recalling Mrs. Gwinne to the remembrance of a former brief meeting. His mother, he believed, had the honour to number Mrs. Gwinne among her friends. Mrs. Gwinne's face softened and she smiled. She was too good a woman to be a snob but nevertheless she was not averse to having her acquaintance with Lady Sidney expanded into friendship. Doing violence to a natural distaste for monkeys, and a prophetic foreboding as to this one, she forced herself to caress Jacob's velvet head and to express her gratitude, on her granddaughter's behalf, for so valuable a gift. Then the coach was found and the ladies handed into it.

"Have you seen the lions at the Tower of London, Lucy?" asked Robert. She shook her head. "Then with your grandmother's permission I will take you there one day."

"It is a bargain?" asked Lucy.

"It is a bargain," he said.

[Adapted from *The Child from the Sea* (1970)]

The Three Grey Men

THE SMALL VILLAGE tucked away in a fold of the Devon Hills was a long way from anywhere, and in the reign of King Charles I did not concern itself much with what was going on in the great world beyond the West Country. It was a world to itself, this West Country world, and the rest of England might have been at the Antipodes for all that the villagers bothered about it, its inhabitants lumped all together as "foreigners" and dismissed from their attention as unworthy of it. Why should they bother themselves with what went on beyond the confines of their lovely land? They were self-supporting. Their rich red earth grew corn in abundance, the cattle grew fat in their green pastures, the orchards that in the spring filled the valleys with a froth of pink and white blossom seemed to flower afresh in the autumn, so bright and rosy were they with their burden of apples. Blackberries and elderberries and sloes for wine were rampant in the hedgerows, and the honeybees hummed all summer time among the honeysuckles and carnations of the old gardens. There were herbs for simpling in the gardens, too, and pumpkins of enormous size, and raspberries and currants for preserves and cordials. Cropping the sweet turf of the round green hills were sheep in plenty to give their wool for spinning and weaving, and in the deep sheltered lanes grew plants for dyeing the wool all colours of the rainbow. And if the women could weave and spin and dye, could bake and brew and distil wholesome waters, the men could plough and sow and reap, could make their own furniture and build their own cob houses and thatch them with golden straw. And if through sickness or bereavement they fell upon evil days there was the squire (in the manor house upon the hill, that ancient manor house that had once been a monastery) to turn to for assistance, or Old Parson in the whitewashed parsonage. And when in the mating and birth and death, at the gathering of the harvest, at the time of the mystical hushed pause of midwinter, and the time of the re-birth of the world a sense of the mystery of things quickened their heartbeats and made them a little afraid, they turned to the old grey church. It had a tall tower that reached like a pointing finger to heaven, a peal of bells that on festival days could be heard miles away, even beyond Paradise Hill, the great green fairy hill with its wishing well that rose up beyond Wildwoods. . . . The whole village loved these bells, and scarcely less precious in their eyes were the other treasures of their church: the beautiful stained glass windows, the ancient golden cross upon the altar, and the fine set of vestments that had come from the monastery, woven in bright colours of gold and emerald, sapphire and amethyst and rosy red. . . .

And in this particular village the church provided not only the setting for those festivals by which the adults gave to the mystery of things some concrete form, but for the children's games as well. It was for the children a nursery full of playthings. It was supposed to be kept locked on weekdays, but the Reverend Obadiah Wilmot, always called Old Parson, put the key behind the mounting block at the lych-gate, and the children knew where it was. And Old Parson knew that they knew; in fact, he had himself pointed out to them its hiding place, and on dark winter days, when not much light came through the stained glass windows and he thought the shadows might make them a little afraid, he would join them at their play and light the candles and tell them stories. He liked children. Indeed being close on eighty, and having had strange fancies in his head ever since that night when his horse had thrown him as he rode through the stormy darkness to a dying parishioner at an outlying farm, he was more than half a child himself. Men tapped their foreheads significantly when Old Parson was mentioned, and the women sighed pityingly and said, "The poor old soul!" when he was suddenly taken with some strange new freak of fancy, such as decorating the churchyard yews with coloured balls to amuse the angels at Christmas, or setting out tempting little meals of honey cakes and elderberry wine on the tombstones for the fairies on midsummer eve. And a few weakly persons confessed themselves afraid of the old man when they met him striding along the lanes in his tattered snuff-stained cassock, his white hair streaming in the wind, talking to himself, cracking his fingers and laughing as though he were having a good joke with someone whom no one could see. "A regular old scarecrow!" was the contemptuous laughing comment of those younger folk who had not known him in the days before his fall, and certainly when his tall gaunt figure was viewed from a distance the simile was apt. But the older people, who remembered him in the old days when his manners and appearance had had a grace that echoed the rarity and sensitiveness of his spirit, did not laugh, and they would rejoice in all that was still left to Old Parson of his old pre-eminence among his fellows. For, eccentric though he might be, he remained a fine artist. No one in the countryside round about could play the fiddle like Old Parson, and no one could carve wood as he did. There was nothing he could not make out of a bit of wood: a spinning-wheel for an old woman, or a cradle for a child; a carved pulpit, or a top; he could still make them all with those fine hands of his. At sight of some lovely thing his eyes would still shine with the old appraising fire, and his voice was still as deep and resonant as ever when from the pulpit he thundered forth the praise of God Who made the world so fair. And he had lost none of his country lore, either. He was still wonderfully handy with sick creatures. Shepherd Joseph, who was the best lambing shepherd in the neighbourhood and spent most of his life in the shepherd's hut on Paradise Hill, always sent for Old Parson to come and help him when his beasts were ailing. Shepherd Joseph had known Old Parson longer than anyone else in the neighbourhood, for he was even older than Old Parson, so old that his white beard reached to his knees, and he never spoke to anyone except to Old Parson, in whom he saw nothing odd whatsoever.

And neither did the children. Like Shepherd Joseph, they were perfectly at home with Old Parson and neither mocked nor shunned nor pitied him. That was because for him, as for them and Shepherd Joseph, a certain door was open and their mutual use of it made them akin. When a child began to laugh at Old

Parson, or run away at sight of him, that was a sign that the child was ceasing to be a child, that the door was slowly closing. Old Parson would go away and weep wildly when a child whom he had loved just turned away from him; it was not for himself that he wept, but for the child.

The playthings in the church would have had few attractions for the modern child, but for these village children, with no nurseries, and few toys, they were a continual marvel. There were not many of them, so that attention was acutely focused, and they were so simple that they left plenty of room for imagination. Instead of the modern nursery wallpaper with its myriad pictures there was in the church only one—a portrait of Saint Nicholas painted in oils upon a wooden board—but so darkened by the smoke of the tallow candles that unassisted by imagination one could make out nothing except the dim sweep of a crimson cloak and the suggestion of a smile upon a bearded face. Then for dolls there was in a niche in the wall, near the wooden pulpit that Old Parson had carved so beautifully, a small statue of the Madonna with her Baby in her arms, so worn by time that the Mother's face was almost worn away and the Child's hand, upraised in blessing, had had two fingers broken off; and a pulpit cloth of cherry velvet embroidered with a small winged cherub with a darn on the nose. And instead of Teddy and Panda there were the dogs on the Crusader's tomb, and these were the best of all, so good in fact that they have a paragraph all to themselves.

They lay at the head and the foot of the tomb. One of them formed a pillow for the Crusader's head and against the other were propped his crossed mailed feet. They were very small dogs of no known breed, for the sculptor who had created them had been a man of humour and imagination and had thoroughly let himself go. The one at the head of the tomb, whom the children called Todd, had a fat, smooth, round body like a sausage, ornamented at one end with a smiling, pop-eyed, snub-nosed, pug-like face, and at the other with a long tail with two twists in it. His legs were quite hidden by his fat body, but his plump little paws peeped out engagingly fore and aft. Percy, at the Crusader's feet, was quite different. He had a fine leonine head, and a grand furry ruff round his shoulders. His body was long and lean, showing all the ribs in a rather painful manner, and he had a bedraggled tail like a moth-eaten ostrich feather. His long front legs, with huge claws on the paws, hung rather dejectedly over the edge of the tomb, but the back ones were folded up very neatly beneath his tail. His eyes were half-closed, weary and sad, as though he still mourned for his master. His was the faithful heart, it was obvious. In real life he would have liked best to lie at his master's feet of an evening, where he lay now, while Todd would have been scurrying round the room chasing the two twists in his tail, or yapping at the door to be let out to his dinner. It was pity for restless little Todd, pinioned beneath his master's mailed head, that had in the first place led Old Parson to spend so many long hours with hammer and chisel, working away until he had got Todd loose, but the delight of the children had been so great when Todd could be lifted out from the tomb and set on the floor and played with, that he had set to work to free Percy too, even though he had realized that freedom was not desired by Percy. . . . For Percy had clung so firmly to the tomb with his hanging forepaws that it had not been possible to chisel them free, and now when he was lifted down he was lifted down without his front legs. . . . Old Parson had grieved deeply over this maiming of poor Percy, until he saw how it endeared him to all the little girls of the village. They were passionately devoted to Percy, loving him if possible even more than they loved the little cherub with the darn on its nose. They would sit beside him for hours, talking to him and scratching him behind the ears, and smoothing his mane with gentle fingers. The little boys, on the other hand, were fonder of Todd. They would take him ratting round the church and knowing his weakness for good living they would bring him apples and nuts, or little bits of pork crackling saved from their dinners.

Saint Nicholas appealed equally to both boys and girls. The mysterious darkness of the picture made it a subject for endless conjecture. Was there, or was there not, something hidden under his cloak? And why was he smiling? Was it because he had some splendid secret to keep? What secret? Had he got it hidden under his cloak? Old Parson wouldn't tell them, however insistently they appealed for information. . . . They'd know all in good time, he said.

The children never played with Mary and the Baby in quite the way they did with Percy and Todd and the cherub, although the little painted wooden statue would have been quite easy to lift out of its niche in the wall, because Old Parson had taught them that this Mother and her Child were holy and not in the same class at all with dogs or even cherubs; but they loved the statue very dearly, and every day the little girls brought nosegays and put them in the niche at Mary's feet. Even in midwinter they always found something they could bring, for the winters were mild in this West Country and there always seemed plenty of scarlet haws on the old thorn tree beside the wishing well on Paradise Hill, and periwinkles or tinted leaves in the deep lanes. And on those rare days when there was snow on the ground they would bring sprays of holly or sprigs of yew. And they would make daisy-chains for Mary's neck, or a necklace of rose hips strung together. And they would bring playthings for the Baby—a chestnut, or a jay's feather, or scarlet moss-cups clustering upon a mossy stick. And taught by Old Parson, who accompanied them most sweetly upon his fiddle, they would sit at Mary's feet and sing lullabies to the Baby.

And of course when Old Parson was up to his crazy tricks, when he was setting out dainty meals for the fairies upon the tombstones or hanging coloured balls upon the yew trees, he always had the enthusiastic co-operation of the children. And at the seasons when the grown-ups were having their games (only they didn't call their festival services games, and drew a sharp distinction, which the children found difficult to understand, between themselves singing hymns in the church on Christmas morning and their offspring singing lullabies to the Baby on ordinary days) the children and Old Parson made the church such a bower of beauty with sheaves of corn, or holly wreaths, or daffodils, or bridal lilies, or whatever the occasion might demand, that people would come from miles round just to look at it. More and more as the years went by the church became an object of pilgrimage for the countryside, and that not only because of Old Parson's eccentricities, but also because of that open door of his; through it a radiance shone that soaked into the very structure of the building where he prayed, so that others liked to pray there too. . . .

And so, for one reason or another, this church had achieved a certain fame, and the Parliament men chose it to make an example of. . . .

Upon a cold grey winter's morning, heavy and still with the coming of snow, only a week before Christmas, when Old Parson was shut up inside the church playing with the children, there rode into the village three grey-faced men dressed in grey garments, with tall black hats. They were ugly men, and about them and their clothes there was a dusty sort of look, as though they had journeyed a long way across some arid desert. Yet tired and dusty though they were they held their heads proudly, as though their tall hats were crowns, as though they knew a lot, or thought they did, and they had about them that unmistakable kingly look that comes from the possession of authority. This suggestion of power, of glooming heavy wisdom, was so blighting that when they dismounted at the pump in the centre of the village and the leader climbed upon the horseblock there to make a proclamation, the usually lighthearted villagers, headed by an unrecognizably grave-faced squire, gathered to hear it in a sober silence.

They had an inkling of what the proclamation was to be about because uninterested though they were in the affairs of "foreigners" they had yet lent an inattentive ear to the reports circulated by travelling pedlars about the goings-on in London lately. They knew that the King and Parliament had fallen out about many things, including religious matters. The King loved the old traditional ways of Catholic worship, the easy colourful ways that were part of the very earth of the easy colourful countryside of England; but Parliament was dominated by men called Puritans who had adopted the teaching of the Dutchman Calvin, a double-dyed "foreigner" in that he was not only foreign to the soil of the West Country but to the soil of England also. Yet those Puritans preferred this way of serving God—a way that condemned every kind of festivity, that ceased to extol the bounty of God and concerned itself only with the terror of hell fire—to that of their fathers, and they had become strong enough to impose the will of

Parliament upon the King. Last Michaelmas, by order of Parliament, it had been commanded that from every church in the land there be removed all deceitful idols, whether pictures, images or painted glass, all coloured vestments, and that no village be permitted any longer to observe the old religious holidays. . . . But who among them had expected that these hated Puritans, who would root out all singing and laughter, all colour and festivity and joy from life, would have thought it worth their while to come all this way to submerge with their dusty greyness this remote fairyland, and to read out their hateful law from the village pump?

Yet so it was. In silence they heard out the proclamation, in silence they gazed balefully at the sour faces of the three Grey Men, and up at the winter sky that today was as drab and cold as the way of life that these men desired to force upon them, and then they sighed and turned homeward again. They did not argue the point. The West Country folk have always been peaceable folk, with a hatred of sharp words. Besides, the Grey Men had the power of the law behind them, and better to lose the few gew-gaws out of the church, old and precious though they were, than to risk the lockup or the stocks. So they just melted away, all except the squire, who thought it politic to stay behind and offer the travellers a mug of ale at his house. . . .

They accepted his offer, but first they demanded to know where they might find the parson. They had not noticed him among the men who had listened to the proclamation and they wished to enforce upon him personally the necessity for obeying the law with thoroughness and dispatch; for on the afternoon of Christmas Eve it was their intention to return and see if their commands had been carried out, and if they had not it would be the worse for the parson and the squire and the whole village. The squire heard their threat and nodded towards the church. "You will find the parson in his church among the so-called idols," he said curtly. "I will await you here." . . .

When they entered upon him, Old Parson was sitting on the steps of the pulpit and at his feet were gathered all the children of the village listening enthralled to the story he was telling them, the story of the flight into Egypt of Mary and her Child. Because it was one of those grey days that made the church dark, he had lit the candles in the big branched candlestick beside the pulpit, and the circle of thin light illumined a scene so lovely that it must surely have melted a heart made of any substance less hard than iron.

Candle-light was always kind to Old Parson. In its radiance his white head shone like silver and his aged face might have been carved out of old ivory. His dark eyes, that at times looked so vacant, were pools of wisdom when he told tales to the children by candle-light, and the expressive gestures of his fine thin hands were an integral part of the telling of the story, as though he painted the scene as he described it. The children, with their bright heads and bright clothes lit by the candle-light, made a glowing mosaic of colour at his feet. Curly golden heads, tousled tow-coloured heads, sleek chestnut and carroty heads, jerkins of russet and green, skirts of rose and blue, of scarlet and primrose and lavender looped up over gay flowered petticoats—it was as though midsummer bloomed again in midwinter. It was not surprising that the cherub with the darn on its nose seemed to smile as it hovered over the scene, and that the Madonna in her niche in the wall beside the pulpit seemed to be holding up her Babe a little higher than usual in her arms, that He might bless it. She too seemed to be smiling, and no wonder, for the children had hung a necklace of holly berries that gleamed in the candlelight blood red like rubies round her neck. Percy and Todd had been lifted down from the Crusader's tomb and sat with the children, enthralled as they were by the astonishing adventures (unrecorded in holy writ) of Mary and Joseph and the Baby on the way to Egypt. Saint Nicholas was half out of the lighted circle, his cloak billowing more mysteriously than ever. It was so dark beyond the circle of the candle-light that the stained-glass windows and the cross upon the altar shone beyond the towering pillars and the interlacing arches like the lights of some distant city seen at dusk through the branches of a forest. Theirs was a faraway celestial beauty but the loveliness within the circle of candle-light had a homely charm that would have sent a truly wise man tiptoeing away back where he came from, lest he disturb the rhythm of a perfect moment.

But the three Grey Men were wise with the wisdom not of the heart but of the brain, and it did not even occur to them to let this moment swing on through time to its perfect completion in eternity. They took it and broke it and flung the broken fragments of it round about them like the petals of a torn flower. They knocked over the candlestick and extinguished the light, so that the cherub and the Madonna and Child and Saint Nicholas fled away into the shadows and the children scattered in fright to the farthest corners of the church, and they seized Old Parson by the arm and pulled him up to stand before them like a criminal in the dock. . . .

Then, one of them prodding him insolently in the chest, they delivered to Old Parson the commands of Parliament, as they had dictated them to the squire and the villagers at the pump: the stained glass must be removed from the windows, the cross from the altar, and all vestments and idolatrous images must be taken away and destroyed. And they themselves would return on Christmas Eve to see if their commands had been obeyed. And when they spoke of idolatrous images they looked about them and saw the children's toys, and one of them tweaked the cherub's nose with a contemptuous finger and thumb, and another snatched at the necklace of holly berries round the Madonna's neck and broke it, so that the berries rolled down upon the floor like drops of blood, and the third, the man who had prodded Old Parson, kicked poor Percy and struck Saint Nicholas with the riding-whip that he carried, and made a dent in the scarlet cloak. . . . But Saint Nicholas made no movement when he was struck, and he did not reveal what he had hidden beneath his cloak, and the Child in His Mother's arms did not cry when the berries fell, nor did the dogs bark or the tweaked cherub so much as flutter its wings in outrage, and Old Parson, when prodded and dictated to, neither moved nor spoke. And the children in the shadows were as silent as mice—more silent, for they did not even squeak.

It was intimidating, this silence, and so was the blazing scorn in the eyes of Old Parson, and for the first time that day the three Grey Men showed slight signs of discomfort. They blustered a bit, but their blustering was swallowed by the deep silence of the church like a stone thrown into deep water, the angry words lost as soon as uttered. One of them rubbed his long nose, and a second coughed, and then they turned on their heels and clanked out of the church rather hurriedly, as though the silence was a physical force pushing them out. When they had gone Old Parson picked up the candlestick, restored it to its place and lit the candles. Then he sat down on the pulpit steps and went on with the adventures of Mary and Joseph and the Baby in Egypt exactly where he had left off, and the children came flocking back from the dark corners to listen to him. ... But it was not exactly as it had been before, because the Madonna's necklace of holly berries lay broken on the floor and the children all had pale faces. ... In the days that followed Old Parson did not remove the holly berries; he left them lying there, like accusing drops of blood, telling how something had been hurt in this place.

3

But that negative action was his only protest. To the squire's astonishment, and secret relief, for he knew the old man's high spirit and had expected some instant explosion, Old Parson made no difficulties when the squire brought skilled workmen to remove the stained glass from the windows; he only asked, humbly and gently, that he himself might be entrusted with the removal of the golden cross and the vestments and the idolatrous images. The squire, looking the old man sympathetically in the eye, nodded. It was his intention to bury the stained glass very carefully in the manor house garden until this tyranny should be overpassed, and it was just as well that they should not have all their precious eggs hidden in the same basket. Old Parson made his request one evening at sunset, when the promise of snow had been fulfilled and the light white flakes were whirling down like goose feathers from the grey sky, and by sunrise the next morning the church looked as bare as Mother Hubbard's cupboard. Everything had gone, even Todd and Percy. Nothing was left except the cross on the altar, and Old Parson promised that that too should have gone by the afternoon of Christmas Eve.

The children wept at first when they saw their empty nursery, but they were cheered by a cryptic remark of Old Parson's. "Remember," he said, "how the Holy Family ran away into Egypt." They did not understand this remark but they found it comforting because in the story Old Parson had told them on the day the three Grey Men came the Holy Family had been having great fun in Egypt. And early on the afternoon of Christmas Eve, a day of sunshine and blue sky and sparkling crystal frost upon the light fall of snow, they almost forgot their grief for their lost toys in the excitement of being summoned by Old Parson to assist him as usual with the Christmas decorations.

"But will the Grey Men like us to have decorations?" asked Prue, the daughter of the innkeeper. She spoke anxiously, for she was the eldest of the children, old enough to understand. . . .

"Holly wreaths are not idolatrous images, Prue," said Old Parson. "We shall decorate as usual this afternoon, and when we have finished we shall praise God by singing in the church just as we always do."

But they did not decorate as usual, for, driven by Old Parson's fiery zeal, they decorated more gloriously than ever before. It was an exceptionally good year for holly and mistletoe and Old Parson had collected masses of it in the church, together with branches of yew and fir, and many strings of the coloured ornaments that he made yearly to hang on the trees in the churchyard to amuse the angels. . . . They were made of inflated bladders, coloured red and blue, gilded fir cones, and the hard outside shells of small round striped pumpkins, and, hung among the green wreaths inside the church, and the yew branches in the churchyard, they were the gayest things imaginable. In the course of the decorating, grown-ups came hurrying along to protest, for like Prue they were afraid that the Grey Men might not like these goings-on, but once they had arrived upon the scene of action their protests died upon their lips and before they knew what they were doing they also were helping with the decorations. They didn't quite know why. It was something to do with Old Parson's compelling power. They got caught in its beam, as a benighted traveller is caught by the finger of light shining across the dark road through an open doorway, and cannot leave it because it is so warm and glowing. And once caught they worked as though their lives depended on it, turning both church and churchyard into a bower of beauty to the glory of God, and when the last holly wreath had been adjusted and the last coloured festoon hung in its place, and Old Parson standing in his tattered cassock at the chancel steps had tucked his fiddle under his chin and struck up the tune of the first carol, men's basses and women's trebles mingled with the voices of the children in the merry air, and the whole village seemed standing shoulder to shoulder within the church. . . . It was only then that the squire, standing close to Old Parson with his head thrown back and his mouth wide open bellowing like an amiable bull, noticed with dismay that the cross was still on the altar.

And a minute later, in the tiny pause between the ending of one carol and the beginning of another, he heard the unmistakable sound of the clip-clop of horses' hoofs on a hard, frosty road. Old Parson heard it too and their eyes met, and the fanatical fire in those of the old man caught up the other into a state of blind obedience that he was never afterwards able to understand.

"Take the cross from the altar and lead straight out of church," Old Parson commanded the squire. "Lead through the village and up through Wildwoods to Shepherd Joseph's hut on Paradise Hill. Go at an easy pace, suited to the eldest and the youngest here." And to the people he cried out in a loud voice, "Follow the cross, good people. Listen to the tune I play and sing glory to God in the highest, and on earth peace. Good will towards men."

When the sun shines in the West Country it seems to shine more brilliantly than in other parts of England. Especially is this so on clear frosty December days. . . . The three Grey Men, not natives of this country, found themselves queerly dazzled by the shining splendour as they rode down the hill to the village. Every rut in the road had its slither of sparkling ice, every humblest weed its diamond crown, every bush its exquisite flowery burden of purest white, and the blue air was shot through with silver and the stillness and the silence held the land so entranced in beauty that time stopped. The Grey Men trotted on bemused, hardly aware of where they had come from or where they were going, or what they were supposed to do when they got there. It was merely mechanically that they dismounted at the lych-gate and passing into the churchyard stood gazing stupidly up at the old yews that were no

31

longer dark and glooming as on the day of their first visit, but silvered with the frost and festooned with spheres of coloured light like a night sky all aglow with the stars and planets. "There's not the smallest orb which thou beholdest, but in its motion like an angel sings." The music was all about them as they stood bemused upon the path, and it was not until the singing procession was almost upon them that they realized that it was not the trees themselves that were carolling so blithely. They looked up and gaped, and so bright was the dazzle of sunshine upon the golden cross the squire was carrying that they faltered, and stepped aside to let it go by.

And before they could recover themselves Old Parson also had gone by playing his fiddle, passing them with a nod and smiling glance that seemed to hold no memory of past injury, but was just the casual greeting of a fellow wayfarer upon the same road. And then the crowd of singing children behind him parted and gathered them in, and as a strongly flowing stream picks up three insignificant straws, so were they picked up and borne onward by the singing village by a way that they did not know to a journey's end that was wrapped in mystery. It was the strangeness of it all that kept them silent, that and the bemusement of the bright light, and the unfamiliar outflowing of good will that brought a strange peace to their hearts. By the time they came to themselves a little they were outside the village, and winding along a narrow deep lane towards the woods, and to have stopped and protested would have been merely to make fools of themselves. Better to go on and see what happened. . . .

4

And so they came to Wildwoods, where the pines and larches grew so thickly together that the sunlight reached them only in shafts of silver piercing like lances through the interwoven branches. They went more slowly now, for they were going uphill, but they did not cease their singing, and the way was easy to travel because the walk through Wildwoods to Paradise Hill was a favourite one with the villagers and the path was well-trodden.

. . . There was a shepherd's hut roofed with pine branches near the bottom of the hill, facing east towards Wildwoods, and Shepherd Joseph spent a large portion of his time there. . . .

The village folk were familiar with the looks of Paradise Hill at sunset . . . and they were familiar too with Shepherd Joseph's hut and the attractive picture it made against the hillside when one emerged from Wildwoods. But the three Grey Men were from a far country, and what they saw when the larches and pines drew back behind them and they were in the open again gave them a shock from which they never afterwards recovered.

When the singing procession came out from Wildwoods the sun was just setting, and Paradise Hill, clothed in a dazzling crystal mantle of white snow, towered up against a sky that passed through every gradation of colour from saffron to rose, and from rose to pale aquamarine that deepened gradually through azure to hyacinth blue, and where the blue was deepest, just above the summit of the crystal hill, one star was shining, and exactly below it upon the hillside Shepherd Joseph's hut was illumined with light from within. The light shone out through the open doorway and made a path of gold over the snow that reached as far as the feet of the Grey Men. A few steps more and they were treading this path of gold, and they were no longer Grey Men weighed down by the foolish wisdom of the spiritual desert where they had been living, but children again walking once more in the light from an open door that they had imagined had shut behind them long ago for ever. They were suddenly young, as young as Shepherd Joseph, young as Old Parson, or as King David when he suddenly let go of his years and dignity and went capering along before the Ark, playing his harp; young as the youngest child in the procession, little Jane the blacksmith's child, riding upon her father's back.

But young though they were, they could not bring themselves to enter the lighted hut, as did those who were children in stature as well as in heart and went crowding in with shouts of glee, tumbling one over the other like ecstatic young puppies for sheer joy that they had found their nursery again. The Grey Men stayed outside with the other grown-ups and looked in through the windows and the door at the heart-warming sight within.

The Virgin and Child might have had to flee away from their home in the church because of the persecution of foolish men, but they were now very much at home in exile, comfortably settled upon a wooden shelf upon the wall that Shepherd Joseph had made for them. His brazier full of glowing coals stood to one side of them, keeping them warm and illuminating the whole hut with rosy light. Upon the other side of them stood Shepherd Joseph himself, leaning on his staff, keeping watch over them as he had kept watch all down the centuries over the weak and helpless. In the straw near the brazier, where in the lambing season Shepherd Joseph put sick lambs to sleep, Todd lay, with Percy stretched out beside him in a most companionable manner. The cherub with the darn on its nose was there too, in reality fastened to the wall, but seeming in the enchanted light to be poised in flight like a real cherub. Indeed, to the children, and to the three Grey Men because a blow dealt by a scene of sudden and unexpected beauty had sent them staggering back into their childhood in an exceedingly dazed condition, the toys in the hut were toys no longer, but living breathing creatures of flesh and blood. If proof were needed of this it was given by Saint Nicholas, who was leaning against the wall beyond the brazier smiling to himself in a most mysterious manner, because his cloak was no longer billowing out over the something secret that he kept hidden beneath it, but lying in deflated folds, and on the floor at his feet was the thing that he had kept hidden—a huge bulging sack. With shouts of joy the children fell upon it because they knew it was for them, and tumbled its contents out upon the floor.

There was a present for every one of them, from the oldest to the youngest, from Prue to little Jane, wonderful toys all fashioned from wood. There were wooden dolls with painted faces and wonderful garments made of gay scraps of silk and velvet, whose colours were strangely reminiscent of the church vestments whose disappearance had been commanded by the Grey Men, wooden skittles for playing the beloved old game of ninepins, wooden figures of rabbits and field mice and little birds all in a row on a branch, wooden cradles for the dolls and wooden hobby horses with flowing manes of real horsehair, wooden tops and Noah's Arks and wooden pipes and whistles for playing merry tunes on.

34

The children did not doubt that Saint Nicholas had had those things hidden beneath his cloak for many a long day, just awaiting a suitable moment for delivery to their rightful owners, but the grown-ups thought to themselves that Old Parson had surpassed himself this time, and no mistake.

When the hubbub had subsided a little, Old Parson, the only grown-up except Shepherd Joseph to enter the hut that night, took the golden cross from the squire and propped it against the wall of the hut beneath the Virgin and Child. "Come now," he said, "the moon is rising and the owls are calling out in Wildwoods that all good children should be in their beds by night-fall on Christmas Eve. You shall come here again whenever you like. This shall be your nursery until the tyranny be over-passed."

5

Afterwards the three Grey Men scarcely remembered how they got back to the village. They only knew that though Wildwoods had been very dark there had been no fear beneath the branches, and that when they had emerged into the lane the stars had shone most gloriously. By the. time they reached the lych-gate the moonlight was so bright that they had refused the squire's invitation to spend the night at the manor house, for the way back to the nearest town would be as clear as though it were day. Yet they lingered a little, loath to leave, and when at last they mounted their horses, the village folk had gone home to bed and they and Old Parson were alone together.

And then the oldest of them said an unexpected thing. "Forgive us," he said.

"There's no harm done," said Old Parson. "The other day you smashed a fine moment in the church yonder, but by God's help I put the pieces together again, and the children took no harm."

Then the second Grey Man, looking up at the fine old church with its soaring tower blocking out the stars, also said an unexpected thing; though the unexpectedness lay not so much in the actual words as in the sadness of the tone in which he spoke.

"Empty windows and a bare altar," he said, "and no colour anywhere when you take the holly wreaths down."

"It will be for a short time only," Old Parson reassured him. "This joyless creed that you are forcing on us is contrary to the spirit of this country and will not endure. In a land where the spring woods are enamelled every colour of the rainbow, where lambs make merry in the meadows and the birds sing as loudly as the choirs of Paradise, you cannot permanently stop the people from following God's example and delighting in colour and music and festivity. Do you think I would have emptied my church of beauty at your orders if I had thought the emptiness likely to endure? I would have died first."

And then the third Grey Man said an unexpected thing; though again the unexpectedness lay not in the words but in the questioning tone in which he said them. "Wassail at Christmas, the blessing of palms, the cross upon the altar and holy water in the stoup—just children's games?"

And now it was Old Parson's turn to surprise his hearers. "Just children's games," he agreed placidly. "Almighty God created us children with the whole wide world for our nursery, and you misunderstand Almighty God, my dear sirs, when you forget at whose command Old Noah made the Ark."

And Old Parson was proved right, for though a bloody civil war had to rage over the land before his faith was justified, yet at long last men and women laid aside the grey garments and the gloomy faces and the hellfire creed that was so alien to the spirit of the land and Merry England was herself again, colourful and light-hearted, praising the bounty of God with the chiming of bells and a merry and cheerful singing in the churches that were filled once again with colour and fragrance and candle-light, and toys for young and old.

"The Restoration" the world at large called this happy period, thinking of that day of jubilation when King Charles II came back to his own again, but the village was as uninterested as ever in what went on in London town, and to them the phrase meant the digging up and replacement of the stained-glass windows, the wearing and embroidering of new vestments, the triumphant return from exile in Shepherd Joseph's hut of the golden cross, the

Madonna and Child, Saint Nicholas, the cherub with the darned nose, Percy and Todd, and the restoration of the children's nursery to its proper place inside the church.

[Adapted from *At the Sign of the Dolphin* (1947)]

The Children and the Painter

Two CHILDREN STOOD gazing at the world over their garden gate. They were just tall enough to rest their chins on top of it, but Jenny, being half a head shorter than Will, had to stand on tiptoe. Behind them the small manor-house where they lived, built of ship's timbers and warm red brick, glowed in the September sunshine, and the garden was on fire with autumn damask roses and marigolds. They could hear the bees humming over the clove gilliflowers under the parlour window, and the soft whirr of their mother's spinning-wheel; for Margaret, their mother, sat just inside the open window with Maria the dog asleep in a pool of sunshine at her feet. Her children were aware of her gentle eyes upon them, and her anxious love. And Will resented it. Jenny, incapable of resentment, nevertheless thought it a pity that love must be anxious, for anxiety was such an imprisoning thing.

It was many days now since she and Will had been allowed outside the garden gate by themselves; and their father had told them that this war was being fought for the liberties of the people. Will kicked the gate, not caring that he stubbed his toe, and Jenny said, "Hush, Will!" for she knew that the angry sound of his shoe against the wood had hurt their mother. The whirr of the spinning-wheel had checked for a moment and she heard Margaret catch her breath. . . . Jenny knew that her mother loved Will more than she loved herself, but this she thought right and natural, for Will was the son and heir.

There was really no reason why the twins should be shut in the garden, but Margaret was always at the mercy of Biddy's tales. Biddy, their cook . . . regarded the war as a godsend. Not only was it a nice change, with the perpetual comings and goings of the Squire and his friends, and the militia drilling on the common and five dead in the first week while they were trying to get their eye trained on the target, but it had provided her with a whole new crop of ogres of a most distinguished type, a pleasing change from the gypsies and tinkers of pre-war days. The Bloody Tyrant and Rupert the Robber were familiar figures now to the children and their mother. Their ghastly appearance was known to them in intimate detail, even down to the twitch in the Robber's left eyelid and the Bloody Tyrant's wet red lips. They knew their habits too, from the boiling down of disobedient little children into soup to the disembowelling of captured prisoners. . . . And they might be here at any moment now, for the war was three weeks old. . . . Margaret and the children took pinches of salt with Biddy's tales, as they had always done, but Margaret found that in time of war salt has a habit of losings its savour.

And so she had confined her children to the garden, though no danger threatened them except from their own militia; and the militia had shelved the war for the moment to carry the harvest. In the country at large little was happening as yet apart from local skirmishes, and in the Chiltern country nothing at all, for here the division was not so much between Royalists and Parliament men as between Parliament men and those whose politics consisted of a passionate desire to be let alone to live their lives in peace. Margaret wished with all her heart and soul that her husband belonged to this latter party. But Robert Haslewood rode with John Hampden, and Margaret's heart was laid open to Biddy's tales.

The children gazed at the common beyond the garden. . . . Will lifted his chin from the top of the gate and pushed it forward in a truculent manner. "Tomorrow," he said, "I shall go into the wood."

"Mother won't let you go," said Jenny.

"Tomorrow Mother has no more authority over me," said Will. "Tomorrow I shall be breeched and next week I shall go to school."

He looked down with loathing and scorn at the childish coat he wore, skirted like a woman's. His breeching had been postponed far too long because through the months of preparation for war his father had been so anxiously occupied, and away from home so much, that even the breeching of a son and heir had hardly seemed important. But tomorrow Robert Haslewood was coming home, bringing with him a sword from London. And tomorrow the tailor would bring Will's doublet and breeches, made to measure on the large side. And the barber would come too, to cut off his curls, and healths would be drunk all round and Will would be a man.

Behind them in the house they heard the opening of the parlour door and the soft voice of little Bess, the still-room maid, saying, "Madam, Madam, the rose jelly is coming to the boil!" The whirr of the spinning-wheel ceased and Margaret rose hurriedly. . . . There was a soft flurry of exit and the closing of the parlour door. The children looked at each other. Their mother's eyes were no longer upon them. . . .

Holding on to the gate, Will suddenly pulled up his knees and shot out his behind, delighting in the rending sound that announced the bursting of gathers. Returning his feet to the ground again he wiped his dirty, earthy fingers all over the fair curls that would be cropped tomorrow, finishing them off on the white collar round his neck. . . .

"I shall have a sword tomorrow," he told Jenny. "And I shall go into the wood now."

"You said you were going tomorrow," said Jenny.

"I shall go now," said Will.

He glanced over his shoulder, but the windows were blank. He unlatched the gate and slipped through.

"Me too," pleaded Jenny. "It won't hurt Mother, for she won't know. We'll be back before the jelly's done. Me too, Will."

"You're only a girl," he retorted. "*You'll* never be breeched."

Nothing stings so sharply as the truth. . . . A lump came in Jenny's throat, but she did not argue with her brother, for Margaret had taught her by example that in humility and gentleness lie a woman's best hope of frustrating the selfish stubbornness of men. She turned away from the gate and walked slowly towards the house. Her gait cried aloud to Will that soon she would have lost her playmate and would be alone. The pain that was already in her heart stirred sharply in his.

"Come on then," he said roughly. "Better come with me than

go snivelling indoors to Mother."

Jenny never snivelled, but again she did not argue. She slipped quickly through the gate and shut it softly. They ran along the rough road that crossed the common until it dipped down into the wood, then left it and ran in among the great beeches where no one could see them. Then they walked slowly, swishing delightedly through the dead beech leaves and savouring the great moment. Will took his sister's hand now, with that air of protectiveness that was always his when he needed the comfort of her stouter heart. It was always eerie in the wood; and nowadays one could fancy Biddy's ogres lurking behind the trees.

Will at eight years old was a plump little boy, stocky and strong, dirty and dishevelled, of wicked intent but not responsible for the gaps in his teeth and the number of freckles across the bridge of his nose. Jenny had shed her first teeth very tidily at an early age and her new ones were all in place, pearly and well-spaced. She was an orderly child. The white apron she wore over her long full-skirted blue dress was spotless, and so was her white cap. Her hornbook hung demurely from her waist. She was smaller than her brother and not at all like him, for her thin face was pale and her hair dark, cut in a fringe across her forehead, fell in soft ringlets on her shoulders. . . . She held Will's hand firmly and soon it ceased to tremble in hers.

When he no longer felt afraid, Jenny's delight in the wood took hold of him. Her moods frequently took hold of him, for they were still very much one child. Reaching for air and light, the beech trees had grown very tall. . . . Below on the floor of the wood the colours showed jewel-bright above the warm russet of the beech leaves. The cushions of moss about the roots of the trees were emerald and there were clumps of small bright purple toadstools, and others rose-coloured on top and quilted white satin underneath. The children stood still, watching. . . . They saw a couple of squirrels and a yaffingale. As they listened the muted autumn music of a deep wood, hidden within its distances, seemed to flow out to them like water from a hidden spring; the rustlings and stirrings of small creatures, the wind that was in the upper air only and stirred merely the highest patterns of the leaves, the conversational flutings of the birds. . . .

41

"It makes my ears feel clean," said Jenny, and Will nodded. His own ears had the same rinsed feeling, but he was inarticulate and would not have been able to find the words to say what he felt. But he had imagination and suddenly it sprang into life. . . . With an airy leap, surprising in one so sturdy, he landed under a dancing beech tree and held out his arms beneath hers, laughter sparkling all over his freckled face. Then he girdled the trunk three times at breakneck speed, calling out to Jenny, "Who am I, Jenny? Who am I?"

She had no doubt as to who he was, for Cousin Froniga had just been reading them *A Midsummer Night's Dream*.

"'Sweet Puck!'" she cried. "'Are not you he?'"

"Come on!" he called to her, leaping off down the slope of the wood.

"'Over hill, over dale,
Thorough bush, thorough brier,
Over park, over pale. . . .'"

His voice died away and Jenny gathered up her skirts and ran after him, her hornbook swinging madly and her cap on the back of her head. The beech leaves crunched gloriously under their feet and the jays began calling again in the depth of the wood. . . . They ran faster and faster, Jenny overtaking Will, and because they had not been in the wood for so long they forgot about the treacherous dip in the ground, like a deep ditch, that hid itself beneath the drifted beech leaves. Jenny fell first, catching her foot in her troublesome petticoats and pitching headlong. Will, running so fast he could not stop, tripped in some brambles and went head over heels after her, yelling with dismay. There was an answering shout from somewhere above them in the wood and both, as they fell, were aware of the man leaping down upon them, the terrible man dressed in black velvet, with pearl earrings and dreadful gleaming eyes and cruel red lips. They saw the forked black beard and the tongue moistening the lips as he sprang. He was just as Biddy had described him. Half dead with terror, upside down among the beech leaves, they shut their eyes and waited for death, for it was the Bloody Tyrant.

"You're not hurt, are you?" enquired a voice. "You fell soft."

Jenny felt herself picked up, carried to the further side of the ditch and set gently down. The owner of the voice returned to the bottom of the ditch and disinterred Will. "Come on, son," he said. "And stop yelling. The little girl never uttered a sound."

Will too was lifted up and set beside Jenny. Shivering with terror they stood there while hands felt them. "No harm done," said the voice. "What's the matter with you?"

Will, though he had stopped yelling, kept his eyes screwed tightly shut, so as not to see the knife, but Jenny opened hers so as to see it, for it was always her way to look hard at what frightened her. There was no knife. She looked up into the face of a smiling, grey-eyed young man with close-cropped hair. He had no earrings in the large ears that stuck out in such a reassuring manner at the side of his head, and he was not dressed in black velvet, but in grey home-spun wool, with a plain white square linen collar such as her father wore. She smiled. Her relief reached to Will and he unscrewed his eyes. His face was not white, but scarlet and burning, and there were tears on his cheeks. He looked at the man, and then, dreadfully ashamed, he hung his head and tried to rub the tears away on his sleeve. But the more he rubbed the more they seemed to come, until at last he was sobbing uncontrollably.

"Will's not breeched yet," said Jenny quickly.

"There's no shame in tears when a man's not breeched," said the stranger. "But what frightened you? The fall, or me pounding along so noisily to pick you up? I'm always a clumsy fool."

"Both," said Jenny. "Will and I thought you were the Bloody Tyrant."

She looked up and saw that he had stopped smiling. He looked both angry and sad. "So you thought I was an ogre?" he said. "It's amazing what feats of transmogrification imagination can perform."

Jenny did not know what he was talking about, but she did think it very odd that she should have seen that dreadful man in black just as clearly as she was now seeing this kindly one in grey.

"Imagination," he went on, "is the greatest power on earth for good or ill. Now then, son, try to imagine you were breeched yesterday."

"I'm being breeched tomorrow!" gasped Will, and hid his shame in the crook of his elbow.

"Tomorrow?" ejaculated the stranger. "Then I've had a lucky escape! If today was tomorrow you'd have drawn your sword and run me through!"

This remark conjured up such a pleasing picture that Will looked up, smiled a little and accepted from the stranger the offer of a severely folded clean linen handkerchief.

"You're painting a picture!" ejaculated Jenny.

"Come and see," said the man, and led the way to where he had been sitting on a fallen tree-trunk at the edge of the wood. A canvas on an improvised easel stood in front of the tree-trunk and was splashed with colour. The children stood and looked at it and the man stood and looked at the children, his merry smile back again about the corners of his mouth and in his eyes. The little boy was merely gaping with astonishment as he stared for what was obviously the first time at a landscape painting, but the little girl was neither gaping nor staring, she was looking, and what she felt shone in her face in a way that touched the man's heart with nostalgic sadness.

Through her eyes he saw his picture, and the world too. He had painted the scene with the whole of his considerable skill and deep delight in the beauty of earth, and it was a good picture of the English countryside in early autumn, but seen now through her eyes the green of that sunlit field had an eternal freshness and the sky, depth beyond depth of blue, was one that would never be clouded. The boy who had become himself had once been as happy as this child in the unconscious conviction that he and his immortal world would never know parting or change. . . .

He stopped looking at his picture and looked at Jenny. He wished he could paint her. . . . He loved these serious little girls.

"You haven't put the sheep in," she said.

"They kept moving, and I'm not clever enough to paint people's portraits unless they stand still."

"Do you paint people's portraits?"

"Yes. I'm a journeyman portrait painter. I travel all over the country, just like the tinkers do, only instead of mending pots and pans I paint portraits."

"Oh!" said Jenny, and her face was transfigured as a brilliant idea came to her. "Would you paint Will after his breeching?

Would you paint him in his breeches and sword?"

"If I did, would your mother give me a silver piece for it?" he asked.

"Mother would give all she's got for a picture of Will," said Jenny with conviction. "And I think Father would give a silver piece."

Will smiled benignly. His distress was now a thing of the past and he was sitting cross-legged on the ground, his red cheeks pleasantly dimpled as he gazed with rapt eyes at the landscape. But he was not seeing the landscape. He was seeing himself tomorrow in his breeches and sword. The painter glanced at him, well aware of what he was seeing. A typical male of the baser sort, none too brave, complacent, happy in the knowledge that his excellent opinion of himself was shared by the females of the family, yet withal a nice though somewhat toothless small boy who might yet make a man if sufficiently maltreated at school. . . . In order to paint the girl he'd be willing to paint the boy too if he kept his mouth shut. . . .

"Are you twins?" he asked.

"Yes," said Jenny.

"Then I won't paint one without the other. Two silver pieces for the two of you."

"That would be wasting Father's money," said Jenny with strong commonsense. "I'm not pretty, Biddy says, and I'll never be breeched."

"Both or neither," said the painter obstinately.

Jenny knew how to deal with obstinate men. Her father was always very fond of his own way, and so was Will. "We'll see in the morning," she said gently. "Will is to be breeched at nine o'clock and afterwards we're going to open a bottle of Cousin Froniga's metheglyn to drink his health. If you come at half-past nine, after the metheglyn, Father is more likely to do what Mother wants than if you came before."

"It will have to be a punctual half-past nine," said the painter, "for otherwise there won't be any metheglyn left for me. Where do you live?"

Will looked up with wide-eyed surprise, for he thought everyone knew where he lived. "At the manor," he said with hauteur.

"My father is Squire Haslewood. My father is coming back from the war just for my breeching."

"It is as yet a leisurely war," said the painter.

Jenny looked quickly up at him, for the laughter had gone again both from his voice and his face. He had been putting some finishing touches to his painting while he talked to them, but now he had stuck his paint-brush behind his ear, his hands hung idle between his knees and he was frowning down at them. . . . Then he came to a decision.

"I'll come," he said. "Hadn't you two better go home now?"

"Yes," said Jenny. "Mother will be anxious if she misses us."

She curtseyed to him carefully, holding out her skirts as she had been taught, her grave face absorbed in her task. He slipped his hand into an inner pocket of his doublet, took something out and handed it to her with a bow. "Take great care of it," he said.

"It's an elf-bolt!" ejaculated Will.

Jenny looked at the little flint arrow-head lying in her palm. She had always longed for an elf-bolt. How many hundred years ago had a fairy loosed this from his bow? Elf-bolts were the most precious of precious things. She looked up at the painter with eyes like stars.

"I found it when I was a boy," he said, smiling at her.

"I'll take great care of it," she said. "Thank you, sir."

"Goodbye, sir," said Will. He too had been well trained and he had a pretty bow. He was not aggrieved that only Jenny had an elf-bolt, though his mouth drooped at the corners. The painter could find nothing in his pockets suitable for Will except a little seal made from a bit of polished red stone. He hesitated, loath to part with the trifle, then gave it to Will. Though commonplace, he was a nice little boy, and the curve of a child's mouth is prettier up than down. The wide half-moon of Will's mouth turned a somersault and his dimples showed again.

"It was given to me by a very brave man," said the painter, "and it will belong to a brave man again once you're breeched."

Will went scarlet, but as he pocketed his treasure he said to himself that he'd keep it always in the pocket of his breeches and then he'd always be courageous; for the crest upon it was a little lion.

46

The children went away and the painter sat listening with his eyes shut until the chiming of their voices had become an indistinguishable part of the music of the wood. The drawing of the one music into the other had been beautiful, as lovely as the fading of prismatic colours into the light, or of the morning star into the blue of day.

[Adapted from *The White Witch* (1958)]

The Hub of the Wheel

WHEN SHE WAS grown-up Stella smiled sometimes when she heard people speculating as to what was their first memory, and seldom able to identify it with certainty. She was in no doubt about her first memory, nor her second, and she knew they had come into her possession on the same day—September the 22nd, 1796, when she was two years old. They were strongly contrasted, and perhaps that was why they had affected her so deeply. The first, though mercifully vague, was none the less dreadful in its terror, and visited her again and again through her childhood, in nightmare or fever, a memory of noise, fire, the grasp of thin arms round her that hurt with the agonising tightness of their grip, then the blackness of water closing over her head. The second was merciful and beneficent; deep silence, starlight shed upon a quiet garden, air that was light and cool upon scorched skin, and then the arms of Mother Sprigg about her, not hard and tight like those other arms but steady and comfortable like Mother Sprigg herself.

"Am I your own girl, Mother?" she asked suddenly when she was ten years old. They were sitting together before the kitchen fire, alone except for the cat Seraphine asleep in her basket with her kittens disposed around her. The candles were lighted and the fire burned brightly, for though it was only the beginning of September the evening was chilly, and Stella was sewing her sampler while Mother Sprigg stitched at her patchwork quilt. It was a fine evening and they had not pulled the curtains; outside the sunset spread a sheet of pure gold behind the beautiful motionless shapes of the old orchard trees, and there was no sound except the whisper of the flames on the hearth, the ticking of the grandfather clock and the soft click of Mother Sprigg's flying needle against her thimble. Stella's needle did not fly and so it did not click. It went slowly and laboriously in and out of her sampler,

48

pursuing painfully the bloodstained path of duty, and now and then ceasing work altogether while Stella sucked her finger and then sprang yet another question upon poor Mother Sprigg.

"Bless the child!" she cried now, and dropped the quilt on her lap. Generally she managed to go on stitching while grappling with Stella's thirst for information, though at times her rosy face puckered with the distress of the intellectual effort, but this question brought her to such a complete full-stop in household activity that Stella gazed at her in round-eyed astonishment. . . .

"Mother?" she queried tentatively.

Mother Sprigg gave her head the sudden accomplished jerk which shook her spectacles (required for close work only) from the bridge of her short button nose to a little lower down, and gazed over the top of them at the child on the stool beside her.

"What makes you ask, love?" she whispered. Yet even while she asked, she knew. The child was old enough now to notice the contrasts; the graceful hand lying on her own clumsy one was only one of many.

"I remember that I came from somewhere else to here," said Stella. "It was quite different."

"What do you remember, child?" asked Mother Sprigg.

"Noise, a fire and black water, and arms that hurt," said Stella in a quick whisper, as though anxious to get it over; and then, slowly and with great sweetness she said, "and after that, Mother, it was quiet in the garden, and your arms were comfortable." . . .

Mother Sprigg's momentary distress passed suddenly in the knowledge that if this question had to come it had come in a good hour. They were alone, and quiet, with the child old enough to be told the truth, yet not old enough, she thought, to feel that distress that only experience of suffering can quicken.

"No, you are not my own girl," she said. "Though the Lord knows you are as dear to me as though you were. Nearly eight years ago, love, you were brought here as a little thing of two years old. Sitting here before the fire, I was, like I am now, patching a shirt, and feeling a bit anxious because father was not back from Plymouth. 'Back at eight o'clock on Wednesday, Martha,' he'd said to me, but the grandfather had struck ten and still I sat there stitching. It was a still night and the strokes of the clock had fallen loud and heavy, like a bell tolling. I was jumpy, I don't say I wasn't. There was an invasion scare that year, and every day we were expecting a landing of the French, and every day the troopships were going off from Plymouth with men and guns for Ireland, for they didn't know where that blackhearted scoundrel Bony would strike, there or here. It was to see Bill his soldier brother set sail on the frigate *Amphion* that your father had ridden to Plymouth. There was to be a grand farewell party on board and your father had ridden off on the Tuesday before it was light, all in a taking because he'd overslept himself and he feared he'd be too late for the grand doings, and too late he was—by the mercy of God."

"Why, what happened?" asked Stella.

"The *Amphion* blew up, love, with the wives and sweethearts and little children of the men all on board. They say a light was dropped by a gunner who was stealing ammunition. A terrible thing it was. Three hundred men and women and children lost their lives, your father's brother among 'em. Your father, riding through Plymouth, heard the explosion, and when he reached the Hoe they were taking the bodies from the water. Your father, he did what he could, and worked as hard as any. One poor young woman whom he helped to take from the water he never forgot. He said she was beautiful, even in death. A sailor had held her up and kept her from drowning but she'd died while he held her— shock, maybe, or some injury—I don't know. She wore a green gown and there was a gold locket round her neck, and her arms were locked tight round the body of her child."

"Me?" whispered Stella.

"Yes. . . . Your father, when he saw you, lost his head. You see, love, we'd had a little girl who'd died at just about the age you were then, the only child we ever had, and your father had grieved over the loss and couldn't seem to get over it. When he saw you there, and a couple of rough chaps unclasping your dead mother's arms from about you, he just snatched you away from them and picked you up in his own arms. One of the men said, 'The child's dead,' but though you were wet and cold like a little fish he knew you were alive. He was in such a taking he didn't answer the man, he just made off with you, without a with-your-

leave or a by-your-leave. There was an inn nearby, and he took
you there and had the good woman look after you, while he went
back to help with the rescue work and see what had become of his
brother. . . . He was not among the saved, was poor Bill. . . . And
the next day, you being as fit as a fiddle by that time, and no one
seeming to know a thing about you, he wrapped you up in his
cloak and rode off home with you. Hour after hour he rode
through the twilight and the dark, knocked nearly silly by the
shock of it all, but you were good as gold all the way and never
cried."

Stella laughed suddenly, her clear happy laugh that was a
delight to all who heard it. Mother Sprigg decided that it was as
she had hoped, though the child was tender-hearted and sensitive
she was too young as yet to realise the tragedy of the story.

"Weren't you startled, Mother, to have father ride home with
me like that?"

"You could have knocked me down with a feather," declared
Mother Sprigg, gaiety springing up in her to answer the laughter
of the child. "I heard Bess trotting in the lane, and I ran out of the
house and down through the garden to the gate. 'Here you are,
Mother,' says father, and he leans down and dumps you in my
arms. You'd been asleep but you woke up then and looked about
you; at the garden and up in my face, and then you cuddled down
comfortable and went to sleep again. The next morning you were
up with the birds and behaving as though you had lived at
Weekaborough Farm from the day you were born."

"And no one ever tried to take me away from you?" asked
Stella.

"No, love. Of course I sent your father back to Plymouth at
once, to make more enquiries, for it was nothing but baby-
stealing, the way he'd walked off with you, but he couldn't find
that you'd any relatives. No one seemed to know who your poor
mother was. There was nothing in her pocket but an embroidered
handkerchief and your little coral, and nothing in her locket but a
curl of dark hair, and a scrap of paper with something written on it
in a foreign language that no one could make head or tail of. Your
father saw her buried decently, and then he put the handkerchief
and the coral and the locket in his pocket and rode off home as fast

as he could to tell me you were ours for keeps, our own girl—Stella."

The child was sitting now with her pointed chin cupped in her slim hands, staring at the fire. She spoke no word of pity for her real mother; it seemed that just now it was the woman beside her with whom her thoughts were busy.

"Mother, was your little girl who died called Stella?"

"No, love, she was called Eliza after my own mother. But your father, being clean besotted about you, must needs choose some fanciful name for you. Star-bright eyes you had, he said, when you first looked up at him, and the starlight was bright on your face when I looked at you that first time, so Stella it had to be, though the name don't go well with Sprigg to my way of thinking. 'But what matter?' said your father. 'The maid will be changing my name for another as soon as she's husband-high, and meanwhile she's my Stella and my sprig of mischief, born on the first of June with candles in her eyes.'"

"And why should I have candles in my eyes because I was born on the first of June? And how do you know that I *was* born on the first of June?" demanded Stella. . . .

"There's no knowing what day you were born, love, but you seemed just over two years when you came to us, and the first of June, 1794, was the Glorious First, when the fleet sailed into Plymouth Sound with six captive French battleships, and in each house a lighted candle was set in every pane. All night they burned, pretty as a picture. Your father saw the sight, and he never forgot it. 'Like all the stars fallen down from heaven,' he said it was; till the dawn came and put them out." . . .

Stella laid her hand on Mother Sprigg's knee and said gently, "*You* are my mother." Then it seemed that she put from her the story for which she had asked, for she smoothed her skirts, looked at her pricked finger, sighed, sucked it, then replaced her thimble and began once more to sew her sampler. Mother Sprigg too picked up her quilt, adjusted her spectacles, and chose a hexagon of crimson velvet with a sigh of relief. . . . It was over, the question and the explanation she had been dreading for so long, and it had all passed off very well indeed. . . .

"I wish it lasted longer," said Stella.

"What, love?" asked Mother Sprigg.

"Just you and me sitting here talking and sewing, with Seraphine and the kittens, and the house loving us."

"Weekaborough Farm," said Mother Sprigg softly. "Your father, he was born and brought up here and he's never left it for more than one night at a time. And I came here as a bride thirty-five years ago and I've never left it for a night and I don't suppose I ever shall."

"I shall," said Stella decidedly. "I shall go to all sorts of places all over the world. But wherever I go Weekaborough kitchen will always be in the middle, like the hub of a cartwheel, and all the roads and seaways will be spokes leading back home."

Mother Sprigg looked at the child sharply. Here was another of the contrasts; this adventurous roving spirit of Stella's was a thing she could not begin to understand. And the child's strange way of talking, always catching hold of one thing and setting it down in the middle of another, like a cartwheel in the middle of the kitchen, a most unsuitable place for it in Mother Sprigg's opinion, made a body's head go round. Yet, apart from her adventurousness, which caused her to go dashing off now and then to goodness knew where in a most disconcerting manner, she was a good little maid who never went roving until she had finished the work which it was her duty to do, and never put things in unsuitable places except in her conversation; and she was to Mother Sprigg the dearest thing in all the world.

[Adapted from *Gentian Hill* (1950)]·

A Chain of Children

Picnic with Albert

COLIN DU FROCQ was paying a visit to Grandpapa and there was nothing he loathed more. It was true that he was accompanied by the girls, but he never had much use for the girls; or thought that he hadn't. To have no brothers was bad enough, he was apt to say, but to have four sisters was worse. . . . Not but what the girls had their uses, especially when he wanted his nails cut.

Why, he demanded of fate, had Father and Mother got to go for a holiday to England? What did they want a holiday at all for? They never did anything to tire them, as far as he could see, and they had five delightful children to keep them amused all day long, not to mention a farm with the proper complement of pigs, cows, chickens and four ducks. The worst of living on a rocky Island in the middle of the English Channel was that the parents could not leave it without being separated from their offspring by miles of stormy sea. . . . It gave a small boy a queer feeling in the pit of the stomach to think that his mother was all that way away.

He sat up in bed rather forlornly and gazed at the grey square of window. Soon, he thought, it would be daylight and then he would feel better. It was a rather chilly spring, and he didn't like the early hours of the morning in chilly weather, for he was one of those energetic sleepers who always kick their bedclothes off during the night, which though good exercise at the time is unpleasant later. . . . He was beastly cold and the room was so big and so gloomy, so different from his dear little room at home. . . . For Grandpapa, the chief doctor of the Island, lived in a large house in the town of St. Pierre, a heavy, wealthy, autocratic, dignified house that was an excellent reflection of Grandpapa himself.

Suddenly Colin wanted his mother so much that he couldn't bear it any more. He leapt from his bed and scuttled across the floor on his bare feet, padded down the passage and burst into the large, depressing bedchamber where slept his two eldest sisters, Michelle and Peronelle, in a four-poster hung with maroon velvet curtains. He took a run and a jump and landed on top of them, then wriggled his cold little body down under the blankets between their warm ones, gaining himself elbow room with vigorous sharp shoves to right and left.

They screamed and awoke.

"It's that young toad Colin," said Michelle.

"Get out, you little beast!" exclaimed Peronelle.

"I want Mother," said Colin.

Instantly the tone of his reception changed. He was given all the room he wanted and his cold toes were rubbed. He was cooed over and even kissed, though only once, because he had a habit of wiping off kisses with the back of his hand that was rather discouraging to the expression of affection. Finally, when it was time to get up, Peronelle came with him to his room to do up his braces and see that he washed behind his ears.

"What would you like to do to-day, darling?" she enquired, for it was the holidays and there was no school, a fact which made the boredom of a visit to Grandpapa more acute than ever.

"I should like," said Colin, "to go for a picnic this afternoon on L'Ancre Common with Albert the Good."

Albert was the donkey who pulled Grandpapa's mowing machine and Grandpapa, for some unknown reason, was devotedly attached to him and most reluctant to lend him to the grandchildren lest he should be overtired; which was only too likely, Albert not being as young as he had been and the grandchildren not as old as they one day would be.

"Well, perhaps," said Peronelle doubtfully. "We'll ask Grandpapa at breakfast," and gathering up the folds of her flannel dressing-gown, and shaking back her long golden ringlets, she went off to a third gloomy bedroom to see how Jacqueline and Colette were getting on. Jacqueline, though older than Colin, still had to be hooked up down the back and Colette, the baby, had been so spoilt that she needed to have nearly everything done for her. Peronelle, the beauty of the family, was also the only practical one and as such had a hard life, for Michelle was intellectual,

Jacqueline was temperamental, Colin was naughty and Colette was both fat and pious, so that none of them could do anything for themselves without disastrous results.

Breakfast was a strained and rather silent meal for Grandpapa's temper, never good at any time and always entirely dependent upon his digestion, was quite shocking after the enforced starvation of the night. Peronelle diplomatically waited until he had absorbed two eggs, four slices of toast, two cups of coffee and the leading article before she ventured to broach the subject of Albert; but even then it was not well received.

"Eh?" said Grandpapa. "What? What? Take Albert for a picnic? Certainly not."

"But Colin is missing Mother," said Peronelle, "and he'd love a picnic with Albert."

"He can picnic if he likes to," said Grandpapa. "You can all picnic and a d—er—good riddance." He stopped for a moment to clear his throat. He always tried very hard not to swear in front of the children, but it was a great strain on him. "But not with Albert. I'll not have that unfortunate animal dragged round the Island like a poodle on a string. I've said so before and I say it again. Why you children can never take no for an answer I don't know. What? What? Just like your mother. Argue, argue, argue about this, that and the other till a man's head goes round."

Grandpapa thumped his newspaper down on the table, wiped his beautiful grey beard and moustache carefully on his silk handkerchief and regarded his four elder grandchildren with early-morning disfavour. . . . A poor lot, he considered, and distressingly like his daughter-in-law. . . . Michelle was both plain and clever, and if there was one thing Grandpapa disliked more than a plain woman it was a clever one; Peronelle, though pretty, was a manager; Jacqueline, though also pretty, was nervous; and Colin was a cheeky young rascal. Only Colette was always dear to him, even in the early mornings, fat Colette with her short fair curls and sky-blue frock, her piety and her devotion to her food. He looked at her affectionately where she sat upon his left hand, eating her sixth slice of bread and honey, her cheeks flushed with health and her eyes still shining with the light of another world that had dawned there while she said her prayers before breakfast. Indulgently he poked one of his fingers through a curl, noting how the morning sun touched it to gold, while Colette, her mouth being used for purposes of mastication, smiled at him with her eyes and reached for the honey.

"Colette would love to have Albert, wouldn't you, darling?" said Peronelle, and gently kicked her small sister under the table.

Colette had been brought up never to speak with her mouth full, so it was a moment or two before she was able to wipe it and give tongue. "Not if Grandpapa would rather not," she cooed.

The others sighed in exasperation. . . . The little wretch was always letting them down like that. . . . She did not mean to, of course, for she was a darling little saint, but like many of the saints she lived so much in the other world that she seldom listened to what people were saying in this one, and also she always spoke the truth, a combination of habits that was bound to lead, sooner or later, to disaster. . . . Uncertain that anything was wrong she beamed upon them all and pursued a straying drop of honey with a long pink tongue.

"Always Grandpapa's good girl," said the infatuated old man, and inserted another lump of sugar in her milk.

"There's Dr. Atkinson starting out," said Michelle acidly, with intent to annoy Grandpapa.

"What? What?" he ejaculated, and hurried from his seat to the window, adjusting his eyeglass and growling savagely into his beard.

Dr. Atkinson was a smart young up-to-date English doctor who had dared to take a house opposite Grandpapa's and set up in a practice that bid fair to rival Grandpapa's own. For thirty years Grandpapa had held undisputed sway over all the livers on the Island and it was not to be expected that he should take this insult lying down. . . . Nor did he. . . . The things that he said about Dr. Atkinson all over the Island were unrepeatable, though naturally widely repeated. It was a fight to the death between modernity and the *status quo* and which would win the Island, watching with deep interest and betting heavily on the odds, did not yet know. . . . It would depend, of course, which doctor General Carew would call in next time he had the apoplexy.

60

(It should be stated here, in parenthesis, that the Carews were the aristocracy of the Island, and General Carew the head of the gang. They were the leaders in society, the supporters of charity concerts and sales of work, and the arbiters of fashion. . . . If you were cut in the street by a Carew you were done for. . . . No more need be said.)

"How early he starts out," said Peronelle wickedly. "He must have a very large practice."

"One of you children ring the bell," choked Grandpapa. "Why are the horses not round? What? What? I should have started on my rounds half an hour ago but for this incessant damnable argue, argue, argue!"

He strode from the room, swearing under his breath, just as Dr. Atkinson in his smart dark-blue brougham drove off down the hill. Ten minutes later the children, crowding together at the window, cheered loudly as the smart dark-green du Frocq brougham dashed up to the door. Grandpapa, his voluminous cape only half on and his top hat on one side, marched out of the house and was heaved in by his panting butler; his black bag of instruments was flung in after him, the door was banged, Lebrun the coachman cracked his whip and the du Frocq horses dashed off in hot pursuit of Dr. Atkinson's inferior animals.

"Hurrah!" yelled the children.

"He's a sporting old boy, you know," Colin conceded, "though he is so d—er—pigheaded about Albert."

"Don't swear, Colin," said Michelle with that elder-sisterly primness which the others found so hard to bear.

"Why not?" said Colin. "Grandpapa does. . . . Now look here, girls, are we taking Albert this afternoon or are we not?"

They retired to the stable to consider the problem. They sat in Albert's manger, and upon that animal's patient but uncommonly hard back, and argued hotly. They were on the whole obedient children but in this case some of them felt that they had a certain amount of justification for disobedience, because Grandpapa had behaved so extraordinarily badly. For one thing there was his hard-heartedness in denying to a child homesick for his mother the consolation of the donkey; and for another thing there was his injustice in complaining of their argumentativeness when absolutely no one had argued a single argue; and for a third thing he had dared to speak slightingly of their beloved mother.

"One doesn't have to obey tyrants like Nero and Grandpapa," said Peronelle at last with flashing eyes.

"Yet Mother said we were to," said Michelle.

"Let's toss for it," suggested Jacqueline.

"Tails take the donkey, heads not take the donkey," said Colin, and tossed.

It was take the donkey. ... Grandpapa would never know because he always continued his rounds in the afternoon and would not be in when the picnic party started.

The old man was unusually chatty at lunch.

In the course of the morning he and Dr. Atkinson, both dashing in different directions after different patients, had collided at a street corner and both the dark-blue brougham and the dark-green brougham had suffered, but the dark-blue brougham had suffered most.

"Wrenched the fellow's right front wheel right off," triumphed Grandpapa, as though this was to his credit.

"How clever of you, Grandpapa," chorused his grandchildren, but he was too absorbed in himself to notice the suspicious charm with which they spoke.

"Shan't be going out this afternoon," he continued, cheerfully masticating underdone roast beef.

"Not?" chorused the grandchildren faintly.

"No. Brougham out of action and weather too chilly for the dogcart. ... Atkinson won't be going out this afternoon either with his brougham in the state it is."

"But he has a dogcart, too," piped Colette. "A beautiful dogcart, bigger than yours."

"What? What?" demanded Grandpapa, masticating Yorkshire pudding. "Nonsense. A cheap, rackety thing. The fellow's never seen in it if he can help it."

"You might both be suddenly sent for," suggested Michelle hopefully.

"What? What?" said Grandpapa, helping himself to his third roast potato. "Not likely. Too early in the year for strawberries and over-eating. .... I'll take another piece of that Yorkshire pudding."

Half an hour later the children, armed with the picnic baskets and hats and coats, again sought the shelter of the stable to discuss the situation that had now arisen.

For the only possible way of getting Albert out to the road was along a cobbled lane that led under the library window, and in the library window sat Grandpapa, his newspaper on his knee, his silk handkerchief spread over his head and his hands folded over his waistcoat. It was true that his eyes were closed and that rhythmical snorts escaped from his well-shaped nostrils, but the sound of Albert's hoofs on the cobbles could not fail to awake him for, like all doctors, he always slept with one ear cocked.

"It's no good," said Michelle, "we must give it up."

"I'd sooner die!" flashed Peronelle.

"Let's carry Albert," said Colin.

"Yes!" they shrieked. "Good for you, Colin!"

"But what if he ee-haws?" asked Jacqueline, one of those tiresome people who always make difficulties.

"We'll tie his mouth up in Colette's flannel petticoat," said Colin.

Colette was divested of her petticoat (a red one, scalloped) and this was done. Then Colin and Michelle took a front leg each and Peronelle and Jacqueline a back one. Colette was instructed to place herself in a stooping position underneath Albert, her back pressing upwards against him, in case Albert, who was stout, should sag in the middle and feel uncomfortable.

"Lift when I say three," said Peronelle. "Now then, you chaps. .... One. Two. Three. .... Help! Would you have believed he was so heavy?"

(A word should here be said, again in parenthesis, about Albert. He was, unlike most donkeys, an absolute angel. Indeed he was very like Colette in disposition, combining as he did placidity and goodness with a certain roundness of form and fondness for the pleasures of the table; perhaps it was his likeness to her that made Grandpapa so fond of him. In colour he was a lovely pearl grey. His ears were long and silky and his nose, because he was not as young as he once had been, snow-white. Because of his years and his tendency to *embonpoint* he moved, as a rule, slowly and with dignity, but he could, when really roused, still go like the wind.)

"My stars! He must weigh a ton!" gasped Colin.

None of the others could speak. Straining, gasping, panting, staggering, they advanced inch by inch along the cobbled way. They came near the library window, they were level with it, they were past it, and then, suddenly, opening his jaws wide and bursting the seam of the flannel petticoat, Albert the Good ee-hawed.

The noise he made was incredible, considering the flannel petticoat. Off came the handkerchief from Grandpapa's head, down went his newspaper, up flew the library window and out came his head.

He made no comment at all. He merely adjusted his eyeglass and gazed, his face becoming congested and his throat swelling a little in his rage. The children lowered Albert to the ground, straightened their aching backs and panted silently, awaiting punishment.

When it came it fitted the crime.

"Pick up that donkey," said Grandpapa, "and take it back where it came from."

"What—carry it?" faltered Michelle.

"Yes, carry it," said Grandpapa. "If you carried it out you can carry it back. I shall be watching you from the window."

"Now then, you chaps," whispered Peronelle. "One. Two. Three."

They returned whence they had come, as they had come, Albert ee-hawing all the way.

They lay flat on their backs on the stable floor, with dreadful pains in their insides after the strain of Albert's weight, and it was quite a long time before they felt better.

Peronelle felt better first.

"Colin," she said, sitting up, "go and see if Grandpapa is asleep again."

Colin, returning, said that he was. . . . Fast, with the newspaper as well as his handkerchief over his head.

"I thought so," said Peronelle. "Anger always sends him off. . . . Now's our chance."

"What for?" asked Jacqueline faintly.

"To carry Albert out again."

"We can't," moaned the others, "we'll die."

"How can man die better than in facing fearful odds?" demanded Peronelle. "Are you cowardly skunks to be ground beneath the heel of a tyrant or are you children of spirit?"

No du Frocq has ever been known, or ever will be known, to refuse the call to action. . . . Silently they arose from the floor.

Now Albert had by this time entered into the spirit of the game, or else he was getting used to things, or else he was simply tired, but anyhow he never ee-hawed. They reached the street half-dead but victorious.

About a mile or so out of the town of St. Pierre the delectable L'Ancre Common stretched from the rising ground, where General Carew's big grey house was, right down to the thundering waves of the Channel. It was covered with coarse grass and crisscrossed by low stone walls where flowers grew, and down by the sea the sand-dunes were dotted with clumps of sea-holly. It was a lovely place to picnic for one could see for miles, the sun seemed to be always shining and the cloud shadows raced over the common like galloping horses.

Two roads crossed the common, the inland road that led past General Carew's house to some farms beyond and the coast road that passed through the little village of L'Ancre, a cluster of whitewashed houses down by the sea where the gardens were full of tamarisk trees and hedges of veronica. This coast road, when it had left L'Ancre behind, swerved inland and joined the other road just beyond General Carew's gate.

The children chose the inland road and tramped merrily along it, singing "Wrap me up in my Tarpaulin Jacket" and leading Albert with Colette and the food upon his back. They felt gloriously happy, for the sky was as blue as Colette's frock and the waves and the wind were singing too.

They felt happy, that is, until they suddenly rounded a bend in the road and saw in front of them a closed gate and a group of ragged little children standing by it. . . . They had quite forgotten the curse of L'Ancre Common—the highwaymen.

Every now and then, across both the roads, were closed gates that separated the grazing ground of one farmer from that of another, and it was the unpleasing habit of the Island ragamuffins to gather in clamorous groups at the gates and demand largesse. *"Des doubles, m'sieur et m'dame,"* they would yell when a carriage drew up at the gate. *"Des doubles! Des doubles!"* and unless satisfied they would leap upon the carriage step, frighten the horses and be as naughty as the sargousets, the Island goblins, themselves.

"There now!" cried Michelle. "Those wretched children! And we can't get over the wall because of Albert. . . . Has anybody any doubles?"

The Island had its own coinage in those days. Eight doubles made a penny, and a franc was tenpence, and the du Frocq children had only six doubles each a week as pocket-money, unless they liked to earn more by collecting snails in the garden. . . . It was a double for six snails.

Everyone's pockets were emptied but they could only scratch up six doubles between the lot of them.

"Why does Grandpapa never fork out anything except on birthdays?" demanded Colin savagely. "He's a mean, stingy old miser. Any decent grandparent would chuck a few doubles about the place now and again. . . . Or a franc piece. . . . He wouldn't miss it."

Colin had reason for his strong feelings for four out of the six doubles were his, for snails, and there is nothing of which one hates to be robbed more than hard-won earnings.

"Cheer up," comforted Jacqueline. "I bet you Grandpapa will tip us before we leave."

"Not he!" snorted Colin. "I bet you anything you like to mention he won't cough up anything at all. . . . Not after Albert."

"Done," said Jacqueline promptly. "Your mummied frog against my bottled snake."

"Done," said Colin.

They reached the gate and instantly the highwaymen were all round them; bright-eyed little rascals with skin tanned a rich brown by the sun, bare legs and feet and bright-hued, ragged clothes. *"Des doubles, m'sieur et m'dames!"* they yelled. *"Des doubles! Des doubles!"*

"Little beasts!" said Colin through his teeth. . . . They did not understand English very well so one could say what one liked.

"Now behave decently, you children," said Michelle to her brother and sisters in her most irritating manner. "If one gives at all one should give with a smile."

"Hold your tongue, Michelle!" said Peronelle. "None of the six doubles are yours, remember, they're Colin's and mine, and it's us to say if we're going to behave well or not, not you."

However, it was not in the nature of a du Frocq not to be generous and the six doubles were handed over to the high-waymen with a good grace, together with a rather stale piece of cake that no one fancied.

The highwaymen, however, were not satisfied, and refused to open the gate. *"Pas beaucoup,"* they said, and spat.

"You're disgusting, greedy little children," said Peronelle loftily. "We have given you our all and you spit. . . . Turn out your pockets, you others."

All the du Frocq pockets were turned out, displaying grubby handkerchiefs and Colin's mummied frog, but nothing else. The highwaymen, appeased, grinned disarmingly—they really were enchanting children—their white teeth flashing in their brown faces. *"Bon jour, m'sieur et m'dames,"* they said. *"Dieu vous garde."*

It is nice to be blest, especially by the poor, and it makes one feel good to be generous, even though one was forced to be, so the children's faces wore expressions of smug satisfaction as they sat eating their tea in a sandy hollow between the two roads.

From where they were they could see the whole landscape. To their right was the town of St. Pierre clinging to its rocky cliff, to their left, down by the sea, the village of L'Ancre, while behind them, sheltered by a clump of storm-twisted trees, was General Carew's house.

When they had eaten everything there was to eat they lay in a happy tired heap blinking at the sun, while Albert the Good cropped the grass and wild thyme and enjoyed himself.

So contented were they that they were half asleep when an unmistakable sound made them suddenly sit bolt upright. . . . Clip-clop, clip-clop. . . . The sound of a horse's hoofs came faintly through the singing of the wind in the grasses and the surging of the waves. Five heads were turned anxiously towards the coast road and there, sure enough, was Grandpapa's yellow dogcart bowling along in the direction of L'Ancre, and Grandpapa himself sitting up beside Lebrun in his tall top hat.

"Heaven help us!" moaned Michelle. "Someone's been taken suddenly ill at L'Ancre. . . . Can he see Albert from there?"

"Down, Albert, down!" hissed the others, and hurried the unfortunate donkey behind a sand-dune.

And then, swift and inevitable as the events in a Greek tragedy, it all happened.

"Look!" cried Jacqueline, and pointed an excited finger at General Carew's house. A maidservant had come out of it and was running wildly towards them, stumbling over the tussocks of grass, the white streamers of her smart cap flying out behind her.

She crossed the first road and came to the children. "The doctor!" she gasped. "I saw him from the window. That's the doctor's dogcart!" and tripping over a tuft of sea-holly she fell headlong.

"Yes," said the children, heaving her up. "Dr. du Frocq. Do you want him?"

"The General!" gasped the distracted girl. "His apoplexy! *Mon Dieu*, I've lost my breath! One of you children run."

Needless to say they all ran; Albert, who hated being lonely, following heavily in the rear.

They came up with Grandpapa on the outskirts of L'Ancre but unfortunately they had reckoned without the nerves of Victoria, Grandpapa's mare, who was a very temperamental lady indeed.

Finding herself charged by five children and a donkey, and seeing a creature with alarming white streamers growing out of the back of her head not far behind, Victoria shied and plunged, tried to recover herself, lost her footing again and fell heavily to her knees. Had not Grandpapa and Lebrun both been stout and

68

heavily cloaked, and so wedged firmly into the front seat, they would have flown over Victoria's head. As it was Grandpapa had a good deal to say.

"But the General, Grandpapa!" cried Peronelle, interrupting his flow of language. "He has the apoplexy. Hurry! Hurry!"

"What? What?" cried Grandpapa, and he lifted his head like an old war horse going into action; as was his habit when any indisposition threatened a Carew.

"Yes, monsieur, if you please," cried the maid, coming panting up to them. "The general's very bad!"

"Drive on, Lebrun!" commanded Grandpapa in ringing professional tones. "Never mind about the woman at L'Ancre. . . . She can wait. . . . General Carew's."

But Victoria was not going to be driven on. She had broken both her knees, was in the throes of a nerve-storm and had no intention of going anywhere except home. She rolled her eyes, foamed at the mouth, kicked and vowed that her back was broken.

'No good, monsieur," moaned Lebrun. "You know what she is."

Grandpapa knew and descended hastily and heavily from his seat, grasping his black bag and growling horribly. . . . He must walk, and he hated walking.

"Never mind, darling Grandpapa," piped Colette. "Let the other doctor go," and she pointed a fat finger in the direction of the inland road.

Eight pairs of eyes—no, ten, for Victoria and Albert looked too—followed her pointing finger and beheld a smart scarlet dogcart bowling along in the direction of the farms. . . . Dr. Atkinson's dogcart, and he was not very far from General Carew's door.

"Thank the good God! The English doctor!" gasped the maid, and was gone like an arrow from a bow.

Colette, of course, was too young to understand that the honour of the du Frocqs was at stake, but the other four understood only too well. Their eyes flew in an agony of affection to Grandpapa's flushed and furious face and they had every sympathy with the language he was using. . . . For though, like all high-spirited

69

families, the du Frocqs did not always see eye to eye, yet at bottom they loved each other and in times of trouble they always showed a united front against the enemy. . . . At this awful moment the children simply adored Grandpapa; and Peronelle's love instantly took the form of practical action.

"Albert!" she cried. "Get on Albert!"

Before Grandpapa knew what was happening he found himself taken charge of by his descendants. He was on his beloved donkey, he found, and bumping along at an incredible pace. He shouted to the children to stop, for he felt the indignity of his position very strongly, but they took no more notice of his forcible language than they would have taken of the buzzing of a bluebottle. Peronelle rushed on ahead, dragging Albert by his reins, Michelle and Jacqueline scampered on each side and Colin, armed with a stick, urged on Albert from behind, all of them shouting like young furies.

"Go on, Albert!" they yelled. "Good old Albert! Albert the Good forever!"

And Albert, in spite of his age and weight, galloped like mad; he laid his ears back, rolled his eyes and simply pounded. Whether he really knew what was expected of him, or whether he wanted to show Victoria that he could do better than she could any day, or whether he was terrified and was running away no one knew, but anyhow he went like the wind.

It was a near thing, and a grand race, for Grandpapa on the coast road and Dr. Atkinson on the inland road were about equidistant from the General's front gate.

Out of the tail of an agonized eye Peronelle saw that wretched maid reach the scarlet dogcart, saw it draw up and saw Dr. Atkinson bend down to hear what she had to say. Then he straightened himself, leaned forward and laid his whip across his horse's back; and his horse was a fine horse and a willing one. . . . Now it's all up, moaned Peronelle to herself, for poor old Albert can't go like that. . . . Perspiration dripped down her forehead and furious tears brimmed over and rolled down her cheeks, but in spite of her despair she did not give up, she ran faster than ever and behind her she could hear the shouts of the others increasing in hoarseness and desperation.

"Stop, you young rascals, stop!" roared Grandpapa, but he was not listened to.

And then Peronelle, her eyes momentarily clear of tears, saw something that she had not noticed before; a second gate across the road between Dr. Atkinson and his objective, and running towards it the very same young highwaymen who had robbed them before tea at the first gate. . . . They had probably robbed Dr. Atkinson at the first gate, too, so they must be making this second attempt simply because they had grasped the situation and had a sporting spirit. . . . Were they going to be little sports? . . . Were they?

A mist once more obscured her vision but a wild shout of triumph from Colin told her that they were. Then her sight cleared and she saw Dr. Atkinson reining in his plunging horse while the crowd of ragamuffins swarmed over the gate and climbed upon the step of his dogcart. *"Des doubles, m'sieur, des doubles, des doubles!"* came their shrill voices on the wind.

That hold-up finished Dr. Atkinson and five minutes later the du Frocq cavalcade galloped in through the General's garden gate.

That evening, by Grandpapa's invitation, the children joined him at dessert, dressed in their best, and found him in magnificent spirits. He gathered them round him, gave them an apple each, chucked them under their chins and told them what he said to the dentist the first time he had a tooth out; the relating of which anecdote was a sure sign of good humour with him and up till now had taken place only on Christmas Day and Easter Day. Colette ·he took upon his knee so that he could poke his finger through her curls and comfort her with sugared figs. . . . For Colette was a little sad. . . . Owing to her tender years and her weight she had not been able to keep up in the great race, though she had tried hard, and she had been obliged to return to Lebrun and Victoria. But she felt much better after the figs and smiled very sweetly as she lay munching with her head on her relative's starched shirt-front.

Grandpapa's good humour was justified, for only a couple of hours before the General had said to him faintly: "You've saved my life, Doctor, you've saved my life," and had weakly but

71

warmly pressed his hand; and as every lightest word spoken by a Carew was always all over the Island by nine o'clock the next morning this meant that Grandpapa and the *status quo* were established for ever. . . . That fool Atkinson, with his ridiculous modern ideas and his chitter-chatter about antiseptics and such like tomfoolery was now nowhere, simply nowhere. . . . Grandpapa polished his eyeglass, adjusted it, and beamed upon Peronelle. . . . How well she had organized the whole affair. . . . And Michelle. . . . She might be plain but he liked her spirit. . . . And Jacqueline and Colin. . . . How those two could shout. . . . All the dear children, he thought, had behaved uncommonly well. What? What? Yes, uncommonly well, and he'd go so far as to say so to their mother on her return.

"Don't you think we ought to go and say good night to Albert?" asked Peronelle, when Colette could eat no more. "After all, we owe everything to Albert."

Grandpapa was in a mood to agree to everything, even though the hour was late and chilly, so they trooped out to the stable, collecting some carrots and a banana—Albert was partial to bananas—from the kitchen on their way.

Albert was refreshing himself at his manger when they came in and was not interested in them until he suddenly saw the banana out of the tail of his eye, when he turned round and reached for it greedily, but seemed anxious not to let the children come too close. . . . His reluctance to allow them near his legs suddenly reminded Grandpapa of the occurrences of the early afternoon.

"How the blazes," he demanded, "did you get that donkey out again?"

"Carried him," they said.

"What? What? A third time?"

"Yes," they said.

Grandpapa was without words, and his face became so congested that the children feared another explosion, but he was only speechless from admiration. . . . The energy, he thought, the determination of these young rascals. . . . It was easy to see whom they took after. . . . They were his very own grandchildren. . . . He plunged his left hand into his pocket, brought up a handful of loose change and gave them two francs each all round.

Silently Colin plunged his right hand into *his* pocket and producing his mummied frog he handed it to Jacqueline with a bow.

[Taken from *Make-Believe* (1949)]

The New Moon

WHAT HAD SHE DONE, thought Rachell du Frocq, to be cursed with these appalling children? She doubted if there was any mother on the Island, or indeed upon any of these islands that lay like jewels in the English Channel, or in England or France either for that matter, who had such quarrelsome children as hers; particularly in the weeks after Christmas. They had been good children before Christmas and angels throughout its exhausting festivities, but now, just when their father had fallen ill and she had her hands more than full, they must turn overnight into complete and utter demons. She looked at them with disfavour as they sat in a row in front of her at the shoemaker's, having new school boots tried on, and wondered from whom they had inherited their vile tempers; not from their father, poor lamb, whose sweetness of disposition not even bronchitis complicated by an overdrawn bank balance had been able seriously to disturb; and not from her, for goodness knew she had the patience of a saint under trials and afflictions that would have ground a lesser woman to pulp; she didn't know who they got them from.

"For goodness' sake, Michelle!" she stormed at her eldest, her magnificent dark eyes flashing and her shapely foot tapping the floor impatiently. "Make up your mind one way or the other. You must know which boots pinch and which don't."

"They *all* pinch," said Michelle, glowering over her spectacles at her mother. "I wish I could wear sandals, like the ancient Greeks. I wish I *was* an ancient Greek."

"Well, you aren't," snapped Rachell. "You are a disagreeable little Channel Island girl of the nineteenth century. And I can't sit here all the afternoon. Hurry up, dear, do. Here are all the rest of you horrid little creatures to be shod before we can get home and have a little peace."

"Now, don't get in one of your rages, Mother," admonished

74

Peronelle, "you'll only make her worse. Keep calm, darling, and think how dreadful it would be if you had ten children to shoe instead of only five."

Rachell began to laugh in spite of herself, and eyed them with less disfavour than formerly; Michelle, plain, bespectacled, and clever; Peronelle, vivid and impulsive, with golden curls framing a heart-shaped face; Jacqueline, dark and pretty and inclined to pessimism; Colin, the only boy, lithe and brown and compact of wickedness; Colette, the baby, round and fat and fair and adorable. . . . Yet to-day even Colette's lower lip stuck out, and her forehead scowled. . . . The exhausted shop assistant put the tenth pair of boots on to Michelle's extended feet, and the quarrel went on again from where it had momentarily left off.

"I tell you there *are* fairies!" shouted Colette.

"There aren't," mocked Colin, "and only silly little babies like you think there are."

"I'm *not* a silly baby," said Colette, and stuck out her lower lip even further.

"If you don't hold your tongue, Colin," said Peronelle, "it'll be the worse for you in another couple of minutes," and she tossed back her curls as a warhorse his mane.

"There are fairies, Mother, aren't there?" pleaded Colette. "You've always said there were."

"Perhaps, darling," said Rachell absently. "Now do be quiet and let poor Mademoiselle get on with the fitting. Your turn, Jacqueline."

"I wish I was dead," said Jacqueline suddenly. The sight of her new school boots reminded her of the return to school next week, and her heart seemed to fall into her stomach.

"Selfish pig," said Peronelle. "Think of the expense your funeral would be to Father."

Colette looked at Jacqueline with large hazel eyes full of reproach. "And Father and Mother love you," she lisped sweetly. "People like to have little girls."

"Conceited little beast," said Colin scornfully. "So you think silly little girls who believe in fairies are nice, do you? Well, they aren't. They're the scum of the earth. I have four sisters, and I should know."

75

Colette wept.

Peronelle, whose special pet her little sister was, leaped to her feet in flaming indignation and flung herself upon her brother. They rolled over on the floor, biting and scratching. Colette, still roaring, flew to Peronelle's assistance, and Jacqueline joined in just for company. Boots flew in the air like hailstones, and the terrified shop assistant leaped for safety like a kangaroo. . . . Only Michelle remained aloof in spectacled superiority. "Something is rotten in the state of Denmark," she observed sententiously.

Rachell arose in her wrath, her worn black dress and cloak swirling around her like the robes of a Cleopatra, and her head held as proudly as though the shabby bonnet that sat on her coiled dark hair were a golden crown. "Stop that instantly," she said, and bending over the combatants dragged them apart with a vigour and skill born of long and arduous practice.

"What a woman!" thought the admiring assistant, picking up boots. "She's like a duchess. She oughtn't to have to wear those shabby clothes and look after those awful children herself."

Rachell, as she shook and dusted her offspring, was thinking exactly the same thing with the part of her mind that lay below the surface and to whose remarks she was generally careful not to listen. She was remembering the days of her youth, the days when she had been the beauty of the Island and had become engaged to Sebastian de la Rue, a man some years older than herself but possessed of dazzling good looks, a pride and temper to match her own, and a fortune that had taken away the breath of her ambitious parents. She had jilted him; thrown away all the great possessions that might have been hers to marry André du Frocq, a penniless poet-farmer whose gentleness and charm had for once in her life bound her pride with chains. She regretted her marriage only on the rare occasions when her strength failed a little under the burden of a delicate husband, noisy children, and that hampering poverty that made her unable to do for them all that she would. Funny, she thought, as she straightened her scowling offspring and placed them again on their chairs, that after all these years she should think again of Sebastian. He had come back to the Island, she had heard, after a successful career in diplomacy, and bought a fine house in this town of Saint Pierre. Had she married him she too would have been living now in a comfortable town house, instead of in that cold farm on a bleak cliff-top, and the governess would have taken the children to try their boots on. ... Ah, but they would not have been André's children, and in none of them would there have been that charm and sweetness (not very apparent just at the moment) that ran like a golden streak through the characters of all of them, and had come to full flower in baby Colette.

The reverie was abruptly interrupted by the discovery that Colette had disappeared.

Colette was a good and a patient child, but there are times when even a worm will turn. Colin's unpleasant remarks about the nastiness of little girls had of course cut her to the heart, but it was not so much the remarks that had sent her rushing out into the street as the sudden hacking away of the roots of her belief. ... Her faith in fairies had been until this moment the foundation stone of her existence. ... She had been one of the true believers, one of those to whom their faith is of such value that beside it all other possessions become a mere encumbrance, and now that it had been taken from her she was a lost soul. It had not been Colin who had destroyed her faith, it had been Rachell with her careless "Perhaps. ..." Colette was old enough to know that one did not answer in that sort of way about what was really true.

Her instinct for flight had carried her right down the street before she knew where she was. The cold winter dusk was drawing in, and the pavements were almost deserted, for most people had gone home to tea. She turned a corner and ran down another street, her small booted feet making a trotting sound on the hard frosted pavement, like those of a sturdy pony, and her plump little figure in its bunchy dark blue overcoat looking as broad as it was long. Fair kiss-me-quick curls framed her face under her scarlet tam-o'-shanter, and larger curls, of the sausage variety, lay in the nape of her neck. Her nose was slightly *retroussé*, and her face was as round and pink as an opened wild rose. She had neither the face nor the figure for tragedy, and no one, to look at her, could have guessed what she was feeling. ... Indeed there were very few people who did not smile as she passed them. ... The passage of

77

Colette through the world was like that; she left smiles behind her, and a lightening of the heart.

Colette's legs, though plump, had always been inadequate to her weight, and presently they ached a good deal and she had a stitch in her side. She had turned two more corners, and she did not know where she was. She stopped, for she was suddenly very bewildered. "Please, God, find me," she demanded, and her eyes went anxiously up and down the street, as though she expected to see her guardian angel rushing along to the rescue.

But she saw instead a smart brougham drawn up at the side of the kerb, outside a tobacconist's shop, with a statuesque coachman, whose face she could not see behind his turned-up collar, sitting on the box staring absent-mindedly into vacancy. It was Grandfather's brougham with its door wide open, gaping for her! With a squeal of delight she scampered to it, scrambled in, and cuddled up in a dark corner, giggling deliciously. Presently her Grandfather, the doctor, would come out of the tobacconist's and get in, and then she would bounce out, and he would roar with laughter into his big beard.

But it was not Grandfather who came out of the tobacconist's, it was an entirely strange footman carrying a couple of long boxes of cigars. He flung them carelessly on to the seat beside Colette, jumped up beside the coachman, and they were off, the brougham swaying and rattling over the cobbles that paved the narrow street.

Colette stopped giggling and began to suck her thumb in some consternation. . . . It wasn't Grandfather's brougham after all. . . . She wasn't frightened, for she was a courageous little girl, but she did wonder where on earth she was going to. She came out of her corner and sat in the centre of the seat; it was so wide that her fat legs stuck out horizontally in front of her, and she found something reassuring in the sight of her muddy boots and scratched bare knees. She always had the feeling that her legs were not part of her but were two friendly little elves who did her bidding and carried her about. Now she waggled them from side to side and dimpled at them, and they seemed to laugh back at her. If the worst came to the worst, they said, they would help her to run away.

78

She felt better now and began to notice the strange magic world through which she was passing. . . . For night had come, the lamplighter had passed like a glow-worm up hill and down dale, and its hour of enchantment was upon this town of Saint Pierre. . . . The black jumble of roofs and chimneys, falling so steeply down the rocky cliff to the sea, were only visible as queer crazy shapes like witches' hands reaching up to pluck the stars out of the sky, and below them the narrow twisting streets were deep clefts in the rock where hobgoblins lurked. The lighted windows of the houses were squares and oblongs of orange and amber and deep scarlet, flowers embroidered on the train of night, while here and there the starlight shone on a sparkle of frost upon a roof or a swirl of mysteriously illumined smoke. . . . Surely in such a world as this there are fairies. Surely news of an invisible world is written plain for all to see in the calligraphy of lights upon the darkness and stars in the sky.

Like the coach that carried Cinderella to the ball the brougham rolled on and on, into the pools of light that lay around the lamps and out again into the darkness that was lapping up between the walls of the houses like the waves of the sea. It seemed hours before it stopped with a jolt beside a door in a wall, with steps leading up to it and a great iron bell hanging down beside it. When the footman jumped down and pulled it, it pealed out menacingly, as Colette had known it would, and she leaned forward anxiously, expecting to see at least a gnome or an ogre come out of the door. . . . For the moment she had forgotten that there were no such things.

But nothing worse came out than a large bald butler.

"Dropped them luncheon visitors in the town, George?" he enquired. "Got them cigars?"

The footman grunted an affirmative and flung open the door of the brougham, disclosing Colette. His jaw dropped, and his eyes bulged so that he looked more like a frog than anything except a frog that Colette had ever seen. "'Ere, Mr. 'Iggins," he gasped. "You come 'ere and 'ave a look at this."

Mr. Higgins came and looked, and so did the coachman. They all three stared with their mouths open, like fishermen who have hooked a mermaid up out of the sea.

"I didn't never see 'er get in, Frank, did you?" said George to the coachman, and the coachman, removing his top hat and scratching his head perplexedly, said no, he was blessed if he had.

'Ask 'er where she come from and take 'er back," suggested Mr. Higgins.

But Colette had no intention of being taken back to where she had come from, for through the open door she had seen inside that house and it was the loveliest house imaginable. At sight of it the spirit of adventure was born in her, and she forgot everything but her desire to get inside. . . . There were great pots of flowers in there; chrysanthemums and tall arum lilies and cyclamens like pink and white butterflies. . . . She wriggled forward so that she could get her legs down, climbed out of the brougham, walked across the pavement and up the steps into the house. It was a full three minutes before Mr. Higgins could pull himself together sufficiently to hurry after her.

He found her standing beside an arum lily, stroking its long velvet tongue with a gentle forefinger.

"And 'oo might you be?" he demanded.

"Colette Henriette Marie-Louise du Frocq," said that lady, and gave him her loveliest smile.

Mr. Higgins was knocked all of a heap. He, together with the footman and coachman, had only recently been imported from England and he could not get used either to the unexpected behaviour of the Islanders or to their outlandish names. Like one in a dream he flung open a door and announced her.

"Mademoiselle Colette Henriette Marie-Louise du Frocq."

Colette walked in.

"And to what am I indebted for the honour of this visit?" asked the tall man who stood on the white bearskin rug in front of the fire.

"I just came," said Colette. "Please may I take my coat off?"

Being the baby of the family, with three adoring elder sisters, Colette was not used to disrobing herself without assistance. She stood holding her arms out wide and looking appealingly up at her host until he realized what was expected of him and came to the rescue. . . . She was so fat, and her coat so much too tight for her, that it was like skinning a rabbit.

"Now my boots," said Colette cheerfully, and sitting down on a chair beside the fire she extended her feet toward him. He was not used to children, and he fumbled clumsily with the intricacy of knots and laces, but Colette was an angel of patience. "You'll do it better next time," she said.

When at last he had got them off he sat down on the chair opposite and looked at her. She wore a diminutive frock the colour of a holly berry, with a white frill round the neck that set off her glowing face like the calyx of a flower. Her toes, stretched out toward the warmth of the fire, wriggled ecstatically in joy at their freedom. She was like a flame burning in his room, a flame of delight.

And Colette in her turn looked at him with all her eyes, for he was to her a new specimen of the human race and as such worthy of her interested attention. . . . She liked people; and she preferred men to women because she found them more obedient. . . . This one was tall and thin and upright, as though he had swallowed a poker and his figure had become moulded to it. There was something rather rigid about his face too, with its hard lines running from nose to mouth, but on the whole he was nice to look at, with crinkles in his grey hair, beautiful clothes, and a peculiarly attractive eyeglass in one eye, attached to his person by a glossy ribbon. Colette decided that she liked him, and smiled.

"Do we have tea now?" she suggested.

The man leaned forward and pulled the bell.

"Muffins," said Colette, "and honey."

"I am yours to command," said her host. Colette beamed again. She liked this man more and more.

"Tea, Higgins," he said, when that worthy appeared. "And muffins and honey."

"We 'aven't got no 'oney in the 'ouse, sir," said Higgins, slightly aggrieved.

"Then send out for it," snapped his master. "Send George."

"Very good, sir," and Higgins withdrew.

There was now an interval, while George fetched the honey, employed by Colette in an account of the history and habits of the du Frocq family. She had not yet discovered that the farmhouse of Bon Repos was not the hub of the universe, round which all

interest centred. . . . And indeed people usually were very interested in Colette's account of what the du Frocq's had had for
breakfast, for it is the personality of the teller rather than the
actual news retailed that gives spice to conversation. . . . And this
man was more than interested. He was thrilled. The very mention
of the word du Frocq seemed to give him an electric shock. He sat
forward in his chair, his clasped hands dropped between his knees
and his eyes fixed upon Colette as though she had brought him
news from a far country. "Yes?" he kept saying. "Yes? And is
your mother well? Five children did you say? And your father ill?
Good heavens! . . . And do they think you're like your mother?"

"No," said Colette. "I'm fair like Father, but I get my fat from
Aunt Sophia Antoinette Marguerite du Putron. . . . She had five
chins."

"Nevertheless," murmured the man to himself. "She is like. . . .
The imperiousness; the habit of command."

At this moment the commanded muffins and honey appeared,
accompanied by pale amber tea in a beautiful teapot of Worcester
china, cream and milk in silver jugs, and sugar cakes upon a lordly
dish; and Colette spoke no more.

She was in the middle of her sixth muffin when she suddenly
burst into floods of tears. The luxuries she had been enjoying, the
lilies and the cyclamens, the muffins and silver jugs and honey-
pots, had for a while made her forget the tragedy of the afternoon,
but now she remembered it and knew these things for what they
were, only the vanities of this world that were but dust and ashes
beside the lost treasure of her faith. . . . There were no fairies. . . .
She howled and howled.

Monsieur de la Rue was deeply distressed. A difficult international situation he could deal with, but a weeping child was
outside his province altogether. But he did his best. He lifted
Colette clumsily upon his knees and implored her to be comforted.
. . . She was comforted. . . . She leaned her head against his
shoulder, and her sobs died away into pathetic hiccups. "Blow my
nose," she whispered. Horribly embarrassed, Monsieur de la Rue
took his beautiful white silk handkerchief from his pocket and
advanced it gingerly toward that *retroussé* member. Colette,
however, did her part. She buried her face in his handkerchief,

made a noise like a foghorn, and the thing appeared to be done. Sighing with relief he put his handkerchief away again and endeavoured to put her down.

Colette, however, did not wish to be put down; she wanted to stay where she was and explain exactly why it was she was so unhappy. The only enjoyment to be got out of affliction, she had long ago discovered, was the telling people about it over and over again, making it worse every time; and lapping up their sympathy as a kitten cream.

And Sebastian de la Rue, the wealthy bachelor diplomatist, a man reputed to be as unimaginative as he was brilliant and as callous as he was subtle, understood Colette as few other people would have done. For he had once lived in a fairy tale. He had once possessed a treasure of such price that the loss of it had turned all subsequent possession to bitterness. He remembered as though it were yesterday a dinner at the Governor's, and Rachell standing before him on the terrace in the moonlight, drawn to her full height, facing a difficult situation with her usual rather cruel directness and grit. "I am sorry," she had said, "but I can't. I never really loved you. You are too proud and too passionate. We are too alike to be happy together." And she had gone away and left him, walking slowly down the terrace with her head held high and the folds of her elaborate white satin evening dress swirling magnificently round her. . . . And he had stood there, looking stupidly at the emerald she had left lying on the palm of his hand, overwhelmed by mental pain so fierce that it had crept through every fibre of his body as though he had been stretched upon the rack. . . . In after years he had come to think that she was right, that a union of two such imperious tempers would have led to tragedy, but that made no difference to the fact that in the full flood of his happiness he had had a shock that had poisoned it for life.

And now the cycle of existence had brought her child to sit on his knee and tell him, through tears, of a fairytale broken.

"Personally," he said, in the cold professional tone that he used at diplomatic meetings of international importance, "I believe in fairies. The evidence to hand in favour of their existence needs sifting and tabulating but to my mind it should be convincing to every man of moderate intelligence." Foreign diplomatists had never been able to tell whether Sebastian de la Rue was lying or not, he had deceived them at will, so it was an easy task for him to bring conviction to one small girl.

"You really, really think there are fairies?" she asked, her eyes fixed on him with her mother's directness.

"I do not hesitate to give it as my profound and unalterable conviction," said Sebastian de la Rue, "that there are fairies. . . . And you can, if you wish, prove the truth of my statement."

Colette's eyes sparkled like stars.

"We are approaching the next new moon," he continued in level tones. "I think I am right in stating that it rises tomorrow." He drew a diary from his pocket, adjusted his eyeglass, consulted it and verified his statement. "Yes. . . . When the moon shines through your window you should salute her as doubtless in common with all other Island children you have been taught to do, and then punctually upon the last stroke of nine you should concentrate your gaze upon the doorstep."

"The fairies will be there?" breathed Colette.

"They may be, or they may not," said Sebastian. "But the gifts of the moon fairies will most certainly be there. The moon never fails to reward courteous little girls who do her reverence and believe in fairies."

Colette dropped her head against his shoulder with a sigh of happiness. "I think," she said, "that I could finish that muffin now."

She finished it and they sat together in the firelight in complete accord for a long time. Then, as a log fell and a shower of bright sparks went up the chimney like a company of stars, Sebastian roused himself and rang the bell.

"You must permit me," he said to Colette, "to send you home in my carriage."

Rachell could make neither head nor tail of Colette's account of the afternoon's adventures. Out of a jumble of arum lilies, muffins, eyeglasses, and someone called 'Iggins nothing very definite emerged except the fact that Rachell herself, by a careless chance remark, had destroyed Colette's belief in fairies, and that an entirely unknown man (not, apparently, 'Iggins), had restored it again by concocting for her a pretty tale of moon fairies and gifts upon the doorstep. Rachell, sitting in front of the kitchen fire and nursing a Colette warm and rosy from her bath, was overwhelmed by penitence for her own misdemeanour and gratitude to the unknown. She had spent a frightful afternoon—they had all spent a frightful afternoon—hunting for Colette, but now, with her precious babe restored to her, and André, tonight, quite definitely round the corner, anxiety and bad temper were things of the past and she was once again the gracious, adoring, indulgent mother whom her children knew best. Colette nestled close, aware that with Mother in this mood, and with a little guile on her part, bedtime could be postponed quite indefinitely.

"What will the moon fairies give me, Mother?" she asked. "Will it be something to eat?"

"Greedy little pig!" laughed Rachell.

"I'm not!" said Colette indignantly. "I should give it all to Father to make him fat."

"Darling little lamb!" said Rachell, and kissed Colette in the back of her neck, under her sausage curls.

Then anxiety overwhelmed her. If Colette, tomorrow night, were to open the front door as the clock was striking nine and find nothing on the doorstep then her faith would be shattered for the second time; and this time for good. It was a difficult problem, this business of guiding the feet of little children as they pattered out of the path of "let's pretend" into the stony road of hard fact. She thought it would break her heart if any child of hers should ever echo Cleopatra's bitter words: "There is nothing left remarkable beneath the visiting moon." For as long as possible the moon must stand to Colette for romance and the radiance of fairy gifts. But would this unknown man see that it did? Would he rise to the occasion that he had himself created?

"You know, darling," she said anxiously to Colette, "if you open the door tomorrow night and find nothing on the doorstep you must not think that means that there are no fairies. The fairies, poor little dears, are very overworked at the time of the new moon, and they can't be everywhere at once."

"Oh yes they can," said Colette, nodding wisely at the fire.

"And tomorrow night there will be lots of things to eat upon the doorstep. . . . There might," she added wistfully, "be enough for me as well as Father."

The night of nights arrived, and Rachell was in an agony. She had half a mind to put some eatables out on the doorstep herself, but there was nothing in the larder that could be spared except the mutton bone and a few stewed prunes, and Colette hated prunes. As the fatal hour drew on her presence was demanded by André, who had now arrived at that stage of convalescence when returning energy takes the form of keeping one's nurse upon the run in a perpetual, but hopeless, search for the right book to suit the mood of the moment. As she ransacked shelves and cupboards, replying patiently, "Yes, darling," to André's querulous "I can't remember the name but you must know the one I mean," her ears were strained to catch the slightest sound in the quiet night that was folding Bon Repos in its peace. . . . At about a quarter to nine she thought she heard a trotting horse, but she could not be certain. . . . And then André upset his supper tray all over the bed, and Colette was momentarily forgotten.

She stood in the middle of the kitchen floor, still dressed in her holly-red dress, for Rachell had said she might stay up as long as she liked. The fire had died down, and there was no light in the kitchen but that of the blazing stars and the new moon. It was one of those great nights of utter stillness when beneath the glory of the sky the earth seems to shrink to a mere nothing, a tiny pensioner crouching at the feet of night. . . . The friendly earth that was to Colette just this little Island, with its rocky cliffs and green lanes a setting for the old farmhouse where she lived in such content, with the sea all round her as a friend by day and night. . . . She could hear it now, a murmuring voice in the darkness. She was not afraid of the sea, not even during nights of storm, for Bon Repos was so near it that its voice was the first thing she had heard when she came into the world.

And now the new moon claimed her attention. It seemed to hang just outside the kitchen window, a thin crescent of perfection whose radiance, added to that of the stars, played with the

86

shadows in the corners of the room and called out answering lights in the warming pans and old copper pots that were ranged round the white-washed walls.

Colette did as all the Island children were taught to do from their babyhood up. She held up her red skirt on either side and curtsied three times to the moon. *"Je vous salue, belle lune,"* she said. *"Je vous salue."*

She was still squatting on the stone-flagged floor, with the faint moonlight pouring over her, when the old grandfather clock began to strike. She stayed where she was, crouched in homage, and counted the strokes on her fat fingers.

"Nine!"

She jumped up and ran like the wind out of the kitchen and down the passage to the front door. When the doorstep was revealed she was so excited that she could hardly see and had to rub her fists in her eyes to clear her sight. . . . Then she saw.

Her shrieks and squeals of joy brought the whole family running pell-mell. André, suddenly deserted by Rachell without a word of apology, sat up in bed and wondered if they had all gone mad, for even for his noisy family the hubbub going on downstairs passed all bounds.

"Grapes!" yelled Michelle. "Both sorts!"

"A bottle of wine!" triumphed Rachell. "Your father may call himself a teetotaller but he loves a little drop of something when it's a duty."

"A jelly!" shouted Peronelle. "A pink one with cherries in it."

"There's a huge bunch of flowers," cried Jacqueline. "That must be for Mother."

"A chicken!" roared Colin. "A chicken in a silver dish, with a sort of white blanket over the top and new moons on it cut out of tomato."

"Come upstairs and show it all to Father," shouted Peronelle.

"A big, big box of chocolates," squeaked Colette, staggering to her feet with the blue-ribboned trophy clasped to her breast. "I don't think, Mother, do you, that chocolates would be very good for Father?"

It was a good hour before the tumult died down and Rachell could clear the children off André's bed and pack them off to their own. It would, she thought, be kill or cure with André, but judging by his alertness of expression and the large quantity of grapes he had already disposed of she fancied it would be cure.

"Lie down, darling, for goodness' sake," she implored him, "while I go and put these flowers in water."

Down by herself in the kitchen she filled a vase for the flowers by the light of the moon. They were flowers such as she loved and had not possessed for years, great white chrysanthemums like balls of snow. She held them between her hands and sniffed their pungent scent with great breaths of delight. Then she untied the ribbon that bound them and found that one end of it was fastened securely to a little box hidden in the middle of the flowers. She opened it and took out an emerald ring.

A stone of elfin green that shone as she held it up to the moonlight. . . . She wondered where she had seen it before. . . . Then she suddenly remembered that scene on the terrace and the tall arrogant girl dressed in white satin. That had been an ignorant girl who did not know what it was to suffer, and the woman of knowledge she had become, looking back at her, hated her for her intolerable cruelty. "And yet I was right," she sighed. "But I need not have done it like that. What a pig you were, Rachell!"

She put the ring on her finger, put her flowers in water and went upstairs to bed.

The next day she went to see Sebastian. André, well through his second bunch of grapes and more than convalescent after a glass of port with his lunch, was not in the least jealous. He was as sure of his wife's love as he was sure that the moon would rise again tonight, and he considered a little sentimentality wholesome for all.

Rachell arrived at Sebastian's front door at about the same hour as Colette had done, when the lighted windows of Saint Pierre were like flowers in the night and the roofs and chimneys were dark shapes that blotted out the stars. She rang the bell with determination and was admitted by Higgins. She swept past him into the hall, her shabby black skirts swirling, and stood for a moment as Colette had done, stroking the velvet tongue of an arum lily, while Higgins cleared his throat, shot out his cuffs, opened the library door, and announced her.

"Madame du Frocq."

Sebastian, adjusting his eyeglass, rose to meet her. He had expected this visit, he had indeed fished for it with his gift of the emerald ring, but now that it was actually upon him he found that he was positively nervous. . . . Shrinking, fool that he was, from a fresh hurt.

Yet, as Rachell put her hand in his, he realized that there was no danger of it, for this middle-aged woman who stood before him was not the Rachell he had known. She was Madame du Frocq, so entirely different a person that she seemed to him a stranger. . . . He realized overwhelmingly how human beings change each other. . . . André du Frocq, with his humility that had softened her pride and his dependence upon her that had called out her tenderness, had made of Rachell a woman she would not have been had Sebastian been her husband. Sebastian had no part in her, and the gulf between them was so wide that they had no further power to hurt each other.

But they had the right to demand of each other a sweet regretful sentiment, enjoyable as the scent of violets in a quiet garden.

"You are as beautiful as ever, dearest Rachell," lied Sebastian tenderly, pressing her hand in its worn black glove.

"Dear Sebastian," murmured Rachell, noting the hardness of his face and mentally thanking God for André, "how good it is to see you again." She paused, lowering her eyes. "I detest," she said, "the cruelty of the girl I once was."

"That," said Sebastian, "is a thing of the past."

The apology over, Rachell sighed with relief, sat down, took off her gloves, and raised her veil. "I hope," she said, "that I have struck the tea hour. I always try to."

Sebastian rang the bell. "Muffins and honey?" he asked with twinkling eyes.

Rachell looked up hastily and a little anxiously. "I do hope," she said, "that Colette was not very greedy the day before yesterday? Yes, Sebastian dear, I adore muffins."

Sebastian stood smiling down upon her, feeling extraordinarily light-hearted. "I may come to Bon Repos and be friends with you all?" he asked.

"But of course," cried Rachell. "It's a funny place, you know. It's very old, and full of children, but the front door is always wide open."

"It sounds like Fairyland," said Sebastian.

[Taken from *Make-Believe* (1949)]

Island Holiday

FOR ENGLISH PEOPLE arrival at the Island was like landing on a foreign shore. It must be some particular arrival that I remember when I think of clearing skies after rain and wind, and of wet cobbles shining in pale yellow sunlight as the cab rattled us away from the harbour. The tall houses of St. Peter Port are built in the French fashion and the streets are steep and narrow. The streets of Wells, where my home was, slope gently so that St. Peter Port seemed to me strangely exciting, more like a grey stone mountain rent with deep narrow chasms than a town. Here and there the chasms were so steep that instead of streets there were long flights of steps between the houses. In the lower part of the town were the exciting shops, dark and foreign, some of them fronting narrow cobbled lanes where only pedestrians could pass up and down. The big covered market was here, and the small stone houses where the poorer people lived. Then, as one climbed, came the bigger houses of the élite of the island. They had steps leading to elegant front doors flanked by tubs of blue hydrangeas or agapanthus, and behind them were gardens where palm trees grew in the mild climate, Guernsey lilies, fuchsias and escalonia. In England we know escalonia as a hedge, or a bush ornamented with rather small sparse sticky flowers, but in Guernsey it grows to a tree and the scent of the many pink blossoms after rain comes in great gusts of perfume.

My grandparents, after their children had grown up, had had a house in St. Peter Port and from the high steep garden one could see the harbour, but I remember it only dimly, for they could not long afford it, and the house I remember so clearly and visited so often was a modern one, beyond and above St. Peter Port. We reached it finally after a last slow drag up the hill and were out in the country, on the flat fields of the hilltop, in sunlight and sparkling air. I believe that hilltop is now completely urban but at

91

the time the row of Victorian villas was lonely and stood out starkly as a sore thumb. But I did not think them ugly. I thought my grandparents' house perfect. The walls were of strong grey granite, and they needed to be for the wind up there could be terrific, and there was nothing but the flat fields between the houses and the cliff edge, and beyond was the sea; and beyond that on clear days one could see a blue smudge against the horizon that was the coast of France. There was a small square of flower garden in front with a bed of mignonette beneath the bay window of the drawing room. Above was a balcony and a passion flower climbed over it and covered the front of the house. It grew as luxuriantly as the mignonette below and the smell of all those flowers in hot sunshine would drift in through the open windows. There was a larger bit of garden behind the house but this was given over to a green lawn where stood the imposing array of instruments used by my grandfather, who among many other things was a meteorological expert, for measuring rain and foretelling the weather.

The cab stopped at the front gate and my grandmother, Marie-Louise Collenette, came out to welcome us. Her face glowed with love but she moved with her usual unimpaired dignity. Nothing ever upset my grandmother's dignity. If her house had started to fall upon her in an earthquake she would have moved out from it in a serene and dignified manner. Had her dignity cost her her life she would have considered death preferable to unbecoming hurry. Like my mother she was a brave woman; I do not think either of them knew what fear was. She was tall and beautiful, with fine dark eyes, and she never lost her slim figure and upright carriage. In my childhood her abundant hair was iron-grey but I have a photo of her when she was very young, showing a mass of dark hair piled in a high crown of plaits on top of her head. She had great charm, and again like my mother no trouble at all in getting her own way. She did not even have to try. She dressed in long full-skirted graceful black dresses, with a black coat and bonnet for out of doors. She always carried an umbrella when she left the house. She had three, one for wet weather, one for doubtful weather, and the third for use on the days when her husband could assure her that it would not rain. . . .

My memories of that arrival stop with my grandmother's

greeting. I recall only being in bed and marvelling at the extraordinary phenomenon of a bed that plunged and rose with the motion of a ship in a rough sea, even though it stood perfectly still on a flat floor. . . .

Driving picnics were still a feature of island life when I was a child. Those who did not possess a brake of their own hired one. If the father of the family could himself drive, he did so, if not a driver was hired with the brake, and the islanders being merry people he enjoyed the outing as much as anyone. Guernsey is a small island and the inhabitants of those days knew it like the palm of their hand. Yet to visit a favourite bay or clifftop six miles away for the fiftieth time brought no sense of stalemate. It was a visit to a well-loved friend and always there was something new to see. And the scenery is varied. The flat sands of l'Ancresse might be in a different country from the rocks of Le Gouffre, and there is no comparing the town church at St. Peter Port with the little church at Le Forêt, where on one of the gateposts was an ancient stone figure of a heathen goddess. And Fermain Bay and Saints Bay have a totally different atmosphere. Fermain was the one the aunts and I visited most often because it was the nearest, but Saints Bay was the one I loved best.

A steep narrow road led down to a few of the bays but others could only be reached by leaving the brake on the clifftop above and climbing down one of the water lanes. I do not know if any of these remain now, and if they do they have probably been tamed and civilised. In my childhood they were steep stony paths, green tunnels arched over by trees, with a stream running down the side under a canopy of ferns. It was wonderful for a child to come out at the bottom and see the stream running across the sand, and run with it to the edge of the sea. Sometimes the picnic would be for both lunch and tea and then mountains of food would be brought and bathing things for everybody, and down in the rocky bay the family would take possession of a cave for the whole day. This sounds a selfish action but there were so few people then, and so many caves, that it was not selfish.

The cave was primarily for the bathers and getting undressed in a cave struck me, aged six, as a stupendous experience. It was also

93

a dignified, leisurely and lengthy one. Edwardian undressing could never be done in a hurry, with dresses fastened up the back with many hooks, petticoats with buttons and tapes to be undone and laced corsets to be removed. And a bathing dress was not put on in a moment. It was an elaborate garment with frilled trousers to below the knee and a short full overskirt. There would be a monumental bathing cap, also frilled, and the whole outfit was frequently scarlet trimmed with white braid. It was a pity it had to get wet. If the mouth of the cave was rather large an elderly female relative who had accompanied the picnic sat at the entrance with a parasol up. Needless to say no gentleman, not even a brother, was allowed to set foot in the cave. They were sent off behind the rocks.

The caves were washed each day by the incoming tide and they had firm floors of silver sand. Frequently they had rockpools in which there were deep crimson anemones, delicate waving pale green seaweed and minute scurrying crabs. The seaweed, or vraic, that clothed the rocks in the bay and was washed up along the shore was lovely too. There was one special vraic called carrageen that was collected at certain seasons and made into jellies and moulds, and another kind used both as a fertiliser and as fuel. Collecting seaweed was called vraicking. A child could be endlessly happy in these enchanted bays, for when one had finished bathing and collecting seaweed and shells there was rock climbing. I was by nature a climber, having a good head for heights, but I liked to climb alone, having served my apprenticeship climbing the cedar tree in the garden at Wells where I was nearly always alone.

I am ashamed now when I think of my furious rages when my aunts interfered with rock climbing. Aunt Emily was easy to shake off for she was no more than a gripper of the ankle. Always so beautifully dressed, she was herself not partial to climbing. With a quick wrench and a quick scramble upwards one could get rid of her. But Aunt Marie, a spare agile person who could climb better than I could, was another matter. If she caught me starting to climb she did not grip my ankle but simply came after me to take care of me. She was the dearest of the aunts but I hated her, and said so, when she shared my rocks. The third aunt, Irene, was

94

seldom in Guernsey for she spent her working life as nanny in royal families abroad. But I know quite well what her methods would have been with disobedient rock climbing children. She could not have climbed, for she was lame as the result of a broken thigh in her childhood, so she would have been an ankle-gripper, but being the most determined woman I have ever known in my whole life she could not have been shaken off. With her free hand twisted in the infant's jersey she would have got that child off that rock, and if there had been any incidents in the process she would have delivered a good spanking. These were her methods with her small royalties, for royal children, she would say, though always lovable and loving, have warm tempers to match. For this reason she liked working in continental palaces for they frequently had tiled floors, and it is easier to empty a jug of cold water over the head of a small boy in a rage than to spank him. He quiets instantly. But you need tiled floors.

My grandmother had yet another method with climbing children. She trusted in God. In early days she once took her young family for a picnic to one of the bays. They were old enough to be left to their own devices, she thought, and being very tired she sat down with a book and began to read. She was disturbed by a total stranger roughly shaking her shoulder. Outraged, she looked up. He was rather white about the gills and pointing with his finger to the cliff. "Are those your children?" he demanded. "If so, take proper care of them." They were climbing high up on the rock face, and they looked very small and were in considerable danger, but they were nearing the top and to shout at them at that juncture would have been the worst thing possible. My grandmother's serenity was inwardly slightly dented but this rude and total stranger must not know it. "I trust my children to God," she said, and returned to her book.

In her old age my grandmother found picnics tiring, but I remember one when she was present and it was illumined for me by the fact that we picked camomile daisies together on the clifftop for the camomile tea she loved. . . .

I had other happy times with my grandmother besides the picking of camomile daisies. When we were alone she often sang to me.

She had a clear and pretty voice even in old age and she knew the ballads of the day by heart. The one I loved best was "Gaily the Troubadour Touched his Guitar as he came Hastening Home from the War". There was another about a lady called Clementine whose feet were so large that herring boxes were the only footwear she could get on. But this one worried me, I was so sorry for her, and I would ask to go back to the troubadour.

The only time my grandfather was really annoyed with me was over my grandmother's singing. It was Sunday evening, the aunts had gone to church, I was in bed and he was enjoying a peaceful and precious evening alone with Marie-Louise. But I had measles, was covered with spots and fractious, and from the top of the stairs I called to my grandmother to come and sing "Gaily the Troubadour". She obediently came rustling upstairs in her Sunday silk but would have nothing to do with the Troubadour because it was the sabbath. However she found a hymnbook and sitting in the armchair in Emily's room, where I also slept, she sang hymns to me. I was enchanted for she had never sung hymns before. In matters of religion she stood midway between her husband's agnosticism and her daughters' faith. I think she was nearer to him than to them, but she did sometimes go to the town church and she did not think it right to sing ballads on Sunday; and she did always just hope that she and Adolphus would not be parted at death. . . .

My grandfather down below was displeased. Not only were hymns reverberating over his agnostic head but he had lost his quiet time with Marie-Louise. Once or twice he came to the bottom of the stairs and called out, "Marie-Louise, come down." But she was not accustomed to being ordered about by Adolphus and replied sweetly but firmly, "Dolph, I must sing this child to sleep. I will join you presently."

I do not know how long it took her to sing me to sleep but I remember my dismay that my grandfather of all people should not have been on my side. Spoilt little brat that I was I thought everyone should always be on my side. Especially with measles upon me.

[Adapted from *The Joy of the Snow* (1974)]

Lost—One Angel

THE YOUNGEST ANGEL was fed up. At five years old he had never really understood what the Nativity play was all about, though plenty of people had done their best to explain it to him, and the rehearsals had wearied him beyond endurance. The angels wore their wings at rehearsals, to get used to them, and his had nearly sent him crackers. The other children's wings stayed put fairly well but his were always twisting crooked or falling off, and he was in perpetual trouble with authority because when a lamb was put into his arms and he was thrust down to kneel in adoration at the foot of the manger he wouldn't adore. Why should he? It was only a doll in the manger and they had a real baby at home. He couldn't see the sense in it, and when it came to the dress rehearsal and he was dressed in a white frock like a girl's, and his newly-washed yellow curls were fluffed out and he was made to look a fool, he decided to quit, and did so just before the scene where he had to kneel with the lamb in his arms and gaze at the china thing as though he liked it. How could he like it when they had a real baby at home? They ought to see the baby up at his place and then they'd see the fools they were to make such a fuss over a thing like that. Full of powerful indignation he roamed round to the back of the stage where it was dark, threw the lamb in a corner, pushed open a door and went out. No one saw him go.

It startled him, when he came out, to find it was daylight still, for in the church hall where the rehearsal was taking place they had darkened the windows to rehearse the lighting. His surroundings were unfamiliar to him, for until today they had rehearsed the play at school. He stood in an asphalted yard. To one side of him there was a big church and in front was an archway in a wall and beyond that was the roar of London on the day before Christmas Eve. He went to the archway and stood there at the top of a flight of steps, looking down at the hurrying people below. He was quite warm for though it was a day with only an occasional gleam of sun it was not cold and he had his winter vest on, and his pants and his new Wellingtons. He had refused to take his boots off and go barefoot like the other angels and as he was such a difficult boy just at present authority had not pressed him, for fear of yells. They hoped he would be more amenable on the night, which was Boxing Day. Everyone understood why he was difficult just now. It was the new baby. He was immensely proud of it but for five years his reign had been sole and undisputed and he could not quite understand the present divided allegiance. And while his mother had been at the hospital he had been sent to stay with Gran, a disciplinarian of the old school, and had suffered much, if deservedly. His small world had been shaken to its foundations and he was much confused.

Where, now, were home and Mum? To the right or the left? He thought, as it happened inaccurately, that they were to the right, and decided he would go down. Step by step he descended, winged and glowing, like Gabriel coming down from heaven with his good tidings of great joy.

Once down on the pavement he trudged purposefully along, his wings crooked as usual and his celestial robe lifted on each side to show his Wellingtons. He aroused a certain amount of curiosity and amusement but no concern, for he appeared to know where he was going and to be happy and content. But when he had passed by he was not forgotten, for his hair was very yellow and his eyes most deeply blue. Some hearts ached at his passing while others leaped with a sense of expectancy. But some people were too self-engrossed, or in too much of a hurry, to notice him at all. They wouldn't have noticed God Himself if they'd happened to collide with Him on the pavement. These pushed and shoved the small angel and once or twice he nearly fell down, but he went doggedly on and gave no sign of the mounting panic in his heart. Once or twice he whispered, "Mum, Mum," but even when he knew he was lost he did not cry. He was a brave little boy.

Mrs. Rodney glanced at the Dresden clock on her mantelpiece and found to her despair that she had fifteen minutes to wait. Her taxi was ordered, her luggage already packed and downstairs, and she had nothing to do. She sat down in front of her empty grate and stared at it. Her service flat was centrally heated but she usually had a small wood fire burning just for the look of the thing. Today, as she was catching an afternoon train to spend Christmas at Brighton, there was only dead ash in the pretty basket grate and it depressed her dreadfully. She was a woman of over sixty but so marvellously groomed that she did not look her age. She had divorced her husband years ago and she had no children. She was well-off and when the immaculate beauty of her flat became intôlerable she travelled. She had very painful arthritis, though she kept it at bay with the latest treatments. She never spoke of her arthritis to anyone because though she had many acquaintances whose parties she attended, and for whom she gave parties in return, she had no real friends. Beneath her accomplished social charm she was a shy woman, and the shining armour that she wore herself intimidated her when she confronted it in others. And everyone she knew seemed to wear it. If shut away inside themselves they were as lonely and scared as she was they gave no sign.

She glanced again at the clock. Ten more minutes. Why should she feel despairing just because she had to wait a few minutes for a taxi, and there was only dead ash in the grate? Nowadays the smallest thing seemed to open up a sort of dry hopelessness within her. And today she was particularly vulnerable because of that dream.

She had dreamed she was back in her childhood, a small girl gazing in ecstasy at the Christmas angel on top of the tree. He was a ridiculous cherub with pink cheeks and yellow hair, made of sawdust and china, with a celestial robe of butter muslin and wings of cotton wool. She thought he was wonderful. The tree was blazing with candles and on it hung presents for them all, but the only thing she wanted was the little angel. The other children were laughing and chattering and pointing at the tree, and the candlelight was reflected in their eyes. Their father was opening his penknife with maddening deliberation, ready to cut their presents from the branches. She was the youngest and she was standing next to their mother, so near that her small hand stole among the soft folds of her mother's dress and she could bury her nose in the bunch of violets that was tucked into her belt. The waits were singing carols outside in the street. Her mother's hand, that had been lying on her shoulder, lifted and caressed her cheek. Then the dream began to pass and she found herself standing back from it all, looking on. She watched the children and their parents, and above all she watched the little girl who was herself. She saw how she leaned her cheek against her mother's hand, and how she gazed up at the little angel at the top of the tree. Then abruptly the scene was blotted out by darkness and she cried out and woke up and remembered that they were all dead.

The dream had haunted her through the day, and above all she had been haunted by the Christmas angel, lost and broken long ago. He seemed to stand for all the lost bliss of childhood, as the empty grate with its grey ashes stood for the present dereliction of her days. Dereliction? What a ridiculous word to use. And she was not sure if she even knew what it meant. It would do her good to spend Christmas at the Brighton hotel. There would be crowds about her and she would have no time to brood.

The hall porter rang through to say the taxi was there and she slipped into her fur coat, that was soft and light as though made of thistledown. Glancing at herself in the mirror over the fireplace she saw a tall slender woman with a delicately tinted face that looked oddly mask-like. As she left her flat and crossed to the lift she asked herself, what else could one do? To wear this mask of beauty was the only form of courage that she knew.

Downstairs Parks, the porter, was already putting her cases in the taxi. When he saw her come out he opened the door of the taxi and stood at attention, his hand to his peaked cap, smiling at her with kindly deference. He had beautiful manners and always made her feel she was somebody still. Very different from the taxi driver, lolling back in his seat with a cigarette dangling from the corner of his mouth. As she crossed the pavement his eyes flicked over her, as though calculating the cost of her pearls and her fur coat. She got in and Parks closed the door gently and tenderly upon her, as though she were something indescribably fragile and precious. She leaned back and then feeling that she would like to wish Parks a happy Christmas she leaned forward again, and just caught the contemptuous wink that he exchanged with the taxi driver.

Somehow it hurt her intolerably to discover that Parks was not what he had always seemed. She supposed he was a socialist, like all the rest. Perhaps he was a communist. She was sure the taxi driver was and an irrational pang of fear went through her. She sat and looked at the jaunty set of his cap and the bristles of hair in the back of his neck, as a short while before she had been looking at her empty grate, and she disliked him intensely.

After a few turnings she saw the beacon of a Belisha crossing ahead and suddenly there was a grinding of brakes all about them and they stopped. The momentary check vexed her. How tiresome it was! At least those wretched pedestrians might have the courtesy to pass quickly and not keep a whole block of traffic waiting interminably like this. Her driver, with no train to catch, was leaning back indolently, uninterested in whoever it might be who was holding them up, but Mrs. Rodney in her exasperation let down her window and looked out, to become instantly aware that almost everyone except her driver was also looking out, or else down from the tops of the buses. Something or someone upon the Belisha crossing was holding them enchanted. For a moment, so unlike herself was she today, she thought the whole of London was waiting and watching, the silence was so extraordinary. Standing up she leaned right out, and with her height was able to see over the low sports car and the errand boys in front of her and get a clear view of the crossing.

The sun had just struggled out through the grey clouds and in a nimbus of glory a small angel was drifting slowly across the street, the traffic banked up on either side of him like the waters of the Red Sea when the Israelites crossed it. An angel in London. An angel on a Belisha crossing. Most people could hardly believe the evidence of their own eyes but Mrs. Rodney instantly recognized him. It was her own angel of whom she had dreamed last night. She could not mistake the little white robe, the fluffy wings, the yellow curls and rosy cheeks. In the charmed silence her conviction seemed to reach to all in the crowd about her and to them too, as their first stunned astonishment passed, he was their own, something lost, something hoped for, something cradled and adored within them. But no one moved or spoke until suddenly the indolent taxi driver caught sight of the heavenly vision. He let out a yell. "My God, it's our Ernie!" The angel passed over, the traffic reared forward again and the quiet moment was swept away as though it had never been.

Beyond the crossing the taxi jolted to a standstill beside the kerb, the driver jumped out and wrenched the door open. "Sorry, lady, I must leave you," he said abruptly. "That was my kid and I must catch him."

"Mine too," said Mrs. Rodney. "I'll help you." And leaving her beautiful pigskin cases unguarded in the taxi she ran with the driver back to the Belisha crossing, and scarcely felt her arthritis. His hand gripping her elbow they crossed over. She did think just for a fleeting moment that she must have gone mad and then in the excitement of the chase she forgot about it. "You go one way and I'll go the other," she gasped breathlessly. "Ask people if they've seen him. He can't have gone far. We'll meet here again."

Half an hour later they met again at the beacon and they had not found Ernie. Mrs. Rodney looked at the driver. His face was white and beads of sweat stood on his upper lip. He was a man of about forty and very ordinary. There was nothing to distinguish him from a thousand others and Mrs. Rodney herself would not have noticed him at all had it not been for their mutual concern for a treasure lost, a concern which in his case was turning into anguish. She saw the misery in his eyes and she saw something else, an experience of life and suffering of which she had never known, and never would know anything at all. She reflected that he was of an age to have served in the war. She also reflected that she herself had spent the war in a comfortable hotel at Torquay. Such reflections were unlike her but she was not herself today. He began to speak quickly and breathlessly.

"Ernie, he's in a play the kids are rehearsing at the church hall this afternoon. Nativity play, they call it. Ernie's an angel. Fed up with it, he is. He's cut and run. But where does he think he's running to? Why didn't he go home? He's in a mood just now is Ernie. The wife's just had a new one and Ernie don't understand it. Been the only pebble on the beach for too long and his mum and I proper took up with him. The wife's not strong yet."

His voice suddenly snapped off and Mrs. Rodney realised that he was in too much distress to know what to do. "We must go back to the taxi and drive to the nearest police station," she said. "A lost angel is a matter for the police I think."

They went back to the taxi, where she never even noticed that her luggage was still miraculously safe, and drove through side streets at breakneck speed to the police station. They went in together, such an oddly assorted couple that the portly sergeant's mouth twitched with amusement as Mrs. Rodney explained the situation. He had had a couple a short while before and in spite of the anxiety of the man before him the humour of the situation was more apparent to him than its potential tragedy. He adjusted his spectacles, drew a sheet of paper towards him and wrote at its head, in a large flowing hand, "Lost—One Angel". He underlined this statement and then asked for particulars. The driver gave them steadily, his name, Bert Thomas, his address and a description of the child.

"Keep your chin up, mate," said the sergeant. "I'll alert the stations and put this statement on the notice board. You'll have the boy back by night, I shouldn't wonder. Bye-bye."

Mrs. Rodney and Bert went back to the taxi. "Your train, ma'am!" he cried, suddenly aghast.

"It does not matter," she said. "I have changed my mind. I do not think I will leave town for Christmas after all. Will you take me back again to my flat?"

They drove back to their starting point and now it was Bert, not Parks, who hurried to open the door of the taxi and heave out the luggage. "Thank you, ma'am," he said simply.

"I hope Ernie will be none the worse for his adventure," said Mrs. Rodney. "You'll soon find him, I know. Goodbye, Mr. Thomas. A happy Christmas to you."

She went upstairs to her flat and did not even notice the dead ash in the grate. She had carefully memorised Bert's address and now she wrote it down in her address book. She knew the angel would soon be found but she would go round tomorrow just to make sure. Would they mind if she took a Christmas present for him and for the baby? She did not think they would mind. What should she take? Trying to decide between this thing and the other kept her pleasantly employed for the rest of the evening and that abyss of hopelessness did not once open within her.

3

There was a Belisha crossing near Ernie's home and when he saw the orange beacon looming up above him his heart gave a leap of joy. He had been feeling dreadfully tired and miserable, and now he was home. But when he had crossed over to the other side he wasn't where he had thought he would be. Yet still he did not cry. He had inherited a great deal of grit from his father and although any frustration of his will made him howl and roar, when things were really bad he was silent.

He turned right and went doggedly on for a couple of minutes until from sheer exhaustion he stumbled and went down on hands and knees. Scrambling up again he turned sideways and there in front of him was a flight of steps. He was back again, he thought, at the place where they were doing the play. It was not home but it was the next best thing. He would not mind being in the play any more now. He climbed up the steps, blind with fatigue, not noticing what was at the top, and went through the wide swing doors, that a few minutes before had been hooked back to allow some luggage to be carried out. Inside was a warm dim sort of cavern so thickly carpeted that the man who was sorting letters inside a glass cubicle to the left did not hear Ernie enter, and he did not see the yellow head so far below the level of his eyes. In front of Ernie, at the back of the cavern, was an oblong of light, the shape of a door. He stumbled towards it and it wasn't a door but an empty box full of light set up on end. He stumbled in and collapsed in a corner. It was warm and quiet and above him in the box was a lamp like a star. He fell asleep and the star shone down on him.

4

Colonel Anstruther walked slowly down the sunny side of the street, even though the sun was not out, just in case it should come out. It was on the whole a rather gloomy day but there were occasional gleams of sunshine. There had been one five minutes ago, fleeting but so lovely that he had stopped and taken his hat off. People had stared at him but he was used to that. He had lived so long and was now so outmoded that people invariably looked at him as though he had strayed out of Madame Tussaud's. It had been such a golden gleam, so gay and reassuring, so tender and amused. It had seemed to bring a profound silence with it, as though all the traffic in London had suddenly been halted, and in the silence he had thought he heard light footsteps running, like the footsteps of a rescuing Child. It was then he had taken his hat off. Then he realised that the silence had been within himself and when he looked about him he could see no child.

He walked slowly on again, very erect in spite of his age, his left hand behind him in the small of his back and his right hand manipulating his walking stick with a slow grace. He was very clean and neat and his clothes had been well made, though they were old and worn now. He wore his hat at an elegant angle and he always had a flower in his buttonhole. He had piercing blue eyes and a snow-white walrus moustache, thought to be the last in London. He lived in lodgings somewhere but it was suspected that they were not very comfortable because he spent a great deal of time at his club, which with the flower in his buttonhole appeared to be his one luxury, for he never took a holiday or went to the theatre. He never talked about himself but it was known he had served in India and in the first world war, and on Remembrance Sunday he appeared with an imposing array of medals on his breast. It was very much feared that he had no income but his pension, adequate years ago but not now. No one knew him very well because his particular brand of integrity would allow him to make no claim upon the compassion of others, and as his need for it grew so did his reserve. But his courtesy never failed. It was slightly impersonal, and as old-fashioned as his hat, but un-tarnishable.

The police station was on the sunny side of the street and he passed it every day without much notice of it, but today a painful breathlessness from which he sometimes suffered came upon him just as he was walking by, and to hide his distress from others he turned towards the notice board. There was a railing beside it which he was able to hold with his free hand. He was better presently, and able to let go of the railing and wipe his forehead with his old silk handkerchief. His sight, still so good that he only needed glasses for small print, cleared again and he was able to bring the notice board into focus. "Lost—One Angel."

Colonel Anstruther was so astonished that he thought he must be making a mistake, and put on his spectacles. Yes, an angel. He read the particulars carefully, registering the address of the child's home in his retentive memory, and was very greatly distressed. Half a lifetime ago he had lost first a small son and then a young wife in India and the loss had left him with a shy yet passionate love for all young children and their mothers. That a mother should be weeping for a lost son at Christmas was to him the very height of tragedy for it was one that he had himself witnessed and endured. He walked on down the street, at first very sadly, and then he endeavoured to turn his thoughts to hope. He did not consider himself a man of prayer but with all the strength that he had he desired and believed that the footsteps of the boy should at this moment turn inwards to a place of safety.

Twenty minutes later he reached his club and paused beside the porter's cubicle in the vestibule to ask if there were any letters for him. He thought there might be as it was Christmas. But there was nothing, not even a card. He reminded himself that there were few people left alive now to remember him. "They are all gone into the world of light," he quoted to himself. He thought that he would go to the library and read for a while, for there was no one about to speak to and the club seemed deserted. He would have liked to have ordered himself a cup of tea but he did not have afternoon tea nowadays. It cost too much.

The lift was beside the library door but as he walked towards it he did not recognize the oblong of light confronting him. He was still a little confused after the queer turn he had had in the street. It looked like a lighted porch leading to unimaginable glory.

"The world of light," he murmured to himself, and he thought he would go in. But at the threshold of the porch he was brought up abruptly, for there was an angel curled up asleep in the corner. A very small one. The starry light overhead shone down upon the yellow head and fluffy crumpled white wings. The round cheeks were flushed with sleep and the long curved lashes lying on them were delicate as gossamer. The shock was so great that Colonel Anstruther was taken again with that rather painful breathlessness. But this time he soon felt better, and the first thing he noted upon recovery was a stout little pair of Wellingtons protruding from beneath the celestial robe. The situation was then clear to him and he went over to the porter's cubicle and said, "Jackson, there's an angel in the lift. I shall be obliged if you will call me a taxi."

Jackson had feared for some time that old Colonel Anstruther was getting a little muddled in his head. His fear now crystallized into certainty. "I'll see to it, sir," he said soothingly, and advanced with slow majesty upon the lift. "Cor!" he ejaculated, coming to an abrupt halt.

"Don't wake him," said Colonel Anstruther. "Call me a taxi and I'll take him to the police station. As I passed I saw on the notice board that there's an angel lost." His voice took on a note of military precision. "Don't stand staring, Jackson. Have you never seen an angel before? Call me a taxi at once."

Jackson did so, and then carried out the sleeping Ernie and put him on the old gentleman's knees in the cab. "Nice little chap," he murmured, and having given the taxi driver his instructions he lingered on the pavement to watch them drive away. He had had Ernie in his arms for such a short while but he would not forget it.

Nor would Colonel Anstruther forget it. The boy was a very solid weight upon his frail knees but he scarcely noticed it. Ernie, half awake but entirely contented now that the atmosphere of extreme devotion to which he was accustomed once more enfolded him, leaned his yellow head with royal condescension against the old man's shoulder and automatically appropriated the flower in his buttonhole. Colonel Anstruther had forgotten that the hair of a clean and healthy child is delicately fragrant. The scent came back to him over the years with very great

PATTERN OF PEOPLE

poignancy, and it made the child in his arms seem peculiarly his own. It was with anguish that he realized that the taxi had stopped and their time together was over. But he gave no sign of emotion and abruptly refusing the taxi driver's offer to carry the little chap, for he looked an 'eavy lump, he took Ernie inside and handed him over to a portly sergeant, who received him into his arms with as much delight as though he were his own grandson. "One angel—found," he ejaculated, and pinched Ernie's cheek with much appreciation. Colonel Anstruther, having ascertained that a police officer would take Ernie instantly to his home in the waiting taxi, refused somewhat haughtily to give his name and address, walked out of the police station and back to his club.

Sitting in the library he felt so tired that he thought he would order himself a pot of tea after all. He couldn't afford it, but it was Christmas. Sipping the hot reviving stuff, and holding the cup in both his thin blue-veined hands because they were trembling slightly after the exertion of carrying Ernie, he realized suddenly that he could not part with the boy. To do so would be like shutting the window in the face of spring. What could he do? The only thing he could think of was that tomorrow, Christmas Eve, he should buy some little gift for the child and take it round. He remembered the address but lest he forget it he took out his notebook and jotted it down. If he were to give up smoking for a month he could get the little chap quite a nice gift. He spent a happy half-hour, the happiest for years, sipping his tea and wondering what it should be.

5

Christmas Eve was clear and blue, and not even the glaring lights of London could quite extinguish the far gleam of the stars. Bert was off duty tonight, and a succulent tea of kippers and buttered toast was just drawing to a greasy but satisfactory conclusion; that is as far as he and Ernie were concerned, Vera his wife had finished some while ago and was sitting by the fire feeding Roy the baby. He was a strong and healthy child with a great deal of fair fluff on the top of his head, imperious manners and a very powerful gift of self-expression. The moments when he was engaged in nourishing himself were much valued for their peace.

Bert lit a cigarette and sat back contentedly. It was warm and comfortable in the kitchen and Vera, the firelight on her face, was looking as pretty as ever he'd seen her. Ernie was beside him, topping off with chocolate. He thought to himself that it needed a jolt such as he had had yesterday to make a man appreciate his luck. He wished he knew who the old boy was who had found Ernie. He'd like to thank him. It was hard not to know who he was.

A rather authoritative knock came at the front door. "It'll be Mum," said Vera, and Bert rose with resignation, for it was Vera's mother, not his, whom they were expecting.

But it was not Mum's downright tones that Vera heard when Bert opened the front door at the end of the passage, but a voice sweet and clear and slightly affected, as ladies' voices mostly were in Vera's opinion. Vera herself was an intensely loving woman but as downright as her mother. Bert, to her horror, was asking the lady to step inside, and for a moment of sheer panic she thought he was going to bring her straight into the kitchen. Then with relief she heard the click of the door of the front room. He'd had that much sense, she thanked God. You never knew with Bert.

Her husband's head came round the door. "It's the old gal who lent me a hand yesterday," he said. "I told you. Wants to see you an' Ernie and the baby. Bring 'em along, Vera."

"I'm feeding Roy," said Vera coldly.

"It don't matter," said Bert. "Come as you are, Roy an' all. She's a married woman and a decent old gal." Then meeting his wife's steely gaze he realized that this was one of the occasions when she was taking after her mother. "Come when you can then," he temporized. "I'll take Ernie."

"He's all over chocolate and kipper," said Vera. "The dishcloth's by the sink."

Bert polished up Ernie and hauled him off and presently Vera, listening intently, heard above the hum of conversation in the next room another knock on the front door, not authoritative this time but humble. Who was it? She did not know but her heart stirred with a strange sense of welcome and she was in a panic because

Bert had apparently not heard the knock. Then it came again, low and gentle, and this time Bert did hear and went to the door. The voice she heard then, so quietly courteous, was one she had somehow been expecting. She had been feeling exasperated but now she felt at peace, and looked down lovingly at the boy at her breast. What was it about him? He was quite an ordinary baby yet people were perpetually coming in and out to see him. It was partly Ernie's doing, of course, always talking about the new baby, but it wasn't only that. She supposed it was because he was new-born just at this time. Christmas set a light about him.

Roy had finished his meal and was now at his best, satisfied, pink, sleepy, silent. She wrapped him in his shawl and took him in the crook of her arm. She was not nervous as she went down the passage for an odd sense of assurance came to her, as though she were a queen. She opened the door and came in smiling, and when she had sat down in the chair that the old gentleman quickly vacated for her she opened the shawl and showed them the baby with a dignity and sweetness that Bert never afterwards forgot.

Ernie behaved beautifully. Clasping to his chest the woolly lamb that Mrs. Rodney had just given him, though he didn't care about it as much as Colonel Anstruther's model aeroplane, he kneeled down beside his mother and gazed at Roy with angelic and selfless adoration. It was a histrionic reflex action, for the woolly lamb was just like the silly thing they'd thrust into his arms during rehearsals, when they'd told him to look and smile and love the baby, and he wouldn't, it being china, but it touched Mrs. Rodney so much that she had to dive into her bag for a handkerchief. She recovered herself in a moment and was eloquent in admiration of Ernie and the baby. While Bert answered her Vera looked up at the tall old man beside her. Their eyes met and she knew that he understood her love for her baby as no one else did, or ever would do, not even Bert.

6

The door had shut behind them and Mrs. Rodney and Colonel Anstruther were alone together in the dingy street. The goodbyes of Bert and Vera had been affectionate and they had been invited to come again and had said they would, so they had no reason to feel shut out. Yet they both suddenly felt lonely and old. The roar of London had an impersonal sound and though the stars were not obliterated by the neon lights it was not very easy to see them.

"I have a taxi waiting," said Mrs. Rodney charmingly. "May I drop you anywhere? I live in Chelsea."

"I shall be most grateful for the kindness," said Colonel Anstruther. He did not feel very easy with her, and the scent of her luxurious soft fur coat and of her perfume oppressed him a little, but he was very tired and he would be glad not to have to struggle home by bus. They walked together to the car, not a taxi at all but a hired Daimler that she occasionally used, and he handed her in and sat beside her. "Anywhere near Chelsea gardens, if you will be so good," he said. From there it would not be too far for him to walk to his lodgings. A quirk of pride made him unwilling that she should actually see where he lived.

Their progress was slow for there were so many cars and buses crowding the streets, so many Christmas shoppers jamming the pavements and the crossings. At first Mrs. Rodney talked brightly of the charm of the little family they had left, and then of whatever else she could think of as a topic of conversation, and Colonel Anstruther did his courteous best to make appropriate replies. But once they had finished with Bert and his family he did not always quite know how to answer for he never went to the Riviera these days, nor to the ballet or the Academy. And so gradually little silences came between them in which both began to be aware of the familiar swaying, tumbling, surging brilliance of the London night sky and the London night streets. They took on added enchantment on Christmas Eve for as the shop windows flashed by there were half-glimpsed tinsel stars and spangled angels, lighted Christmas trees and bunches of holly. The people surging along the pavements were excited and happy, and among them were a great many bright-eyed children clutching parcels done up in coloured paper. The familiar hot petrol stench of dried-up London came in through the windows freshened by the scent of oranges and greenery, and, now and again, flowers. Mrs. Rodney found it all very moving tonight. Colonel Anstruther saw it as though it was a curtain swaying in the wind, or a passing dream. What was real to him was the picture of Vera looking up at him, and understanding that he understood. The whole of London seemed only to exist tonight because of Vera with Roy in her arms.

The car swung away from the busy streets and glided down a quieter one towards the river, and again came the scent of flowers. Colonel Anstruther spoke to the chauffeur through the speaking tube, and when the car stopped he murmured a word of apology to Mrs. Rodney and got out and went into the flower shop. Inside he bought a bunch of violets and coming back to the car again he gave them to her, courteously wishing her a happy Christmas. Behind her laughing chatter and the make-up on her face he had been from the beginning aware of great desolation but also of a matching courage. Though he did not feel at ease with this woman he could admire her. But when the tears came into her eyes, and she could not find the words to thank him, he thought perhaps he had made a mistake to give her violets. A couple of heartless orchids would have been better. Violets are too nostalgic.

On the embankment, where the lights gleamed on the dark water, they stopped again and he got out and lifted his hat to say goodbye, but she said, "I will get out for a moment. It is so cool and fresh here." They walked a few paces together and then stopped, and though London roared behind them it seemed strangely quiet. In the quiet they heard clocks striking and the voice of the river flowing by; and Colonel Anstruther thought he heard again the running footsteps of the rescuing Child. Then Mrs. Rodney asked, scarcely above her breath, "Is it true?"

He knew what was in her mind and turning to her he answered gently, "I believe so. I believe there is a mystery burning like a light behind the appearance of things. Or you could say it is a peace at the heart of our tumult. On such a day as this moments of quiet take us by surprise. Have you not found it so?"

She said, "Can dreams of the happy past be more than memory?"

He answered, "Why not? There is no time in dreams. They can just as well be indications of the future."

They walked back to the car and when he had thanked her and said goodbye he stood waiting, hat in hand, for her to get in. With her foot on the step she turned back to him and said shyly, "I do not like to say goodbye. Can you lunch with me one day?"

He had finished with such social occasions, he had thought and hoped, but he realized suddenly, with grateful humility, that the power of succour was not yet dead in him. Knowing this he could do no other than thank her and give her his card, with the address of his club upon it. Then he stepped back and she got in and the car glided on. Looking back at him she saw that he was a very old man, older than she had thought, but she knew with a sense of strength and comfort that his wisdom would be all the greater for her need.

[Taken from *The Lost Angel* (1971)]

Looking at the Little Things

SHE WAS DRIVING with her father in a pony trap along a country lane bordered on each side with trees. They were like no trees she had ever seen in the London parks, they were tremendous, august and unearthly. Far up in the blue sky there was a faint rustling of leaves, a movement of branches in the May wind, but below there was a motionless, shadowed, possessive stillness. Yet though she pressed closer to her father she was not afraid of them. She thought they were good trees, pleased to see her and glad her father was taking her to see her namesake, Cousin Mary Lindsay. She had not been called after her cousin on purpose, she had understood from talk between her father and mother, merely by accident; but poor Cousin Mary had been so pleased to have a child of the family bearing her name that they had not liked to undeceive her. And now she had asked that the little Mary might be brought to see her so that she could show her "the little things". She had sent the trap from the pub to meet the London train at the nearest station, six miles away. There was a boy at the pub who could drive it. . . .

There was a village green with thatched cottages about it, one of them the village shop and post office, and opposite the lych-gate of the church lilacs grew in a tangled mass behind a garden wall. In the wall was a green door under a stone archway. It had a round brass handle and beside it was an ancient rusted iron bellpull. Cut into the stone on the other side of the arch was the name of the house. It was called The Laurels, though there wasn't a laurel in sight. The lilacs had grown so tall that their branches hung over the wall and over the arch above the door. Four steps led up to the door and they were very worn in the middle. What could be behind the door Mary couldn't imagine. Not the world she knew. The thicket of purple and white blossom, the door and the steps, were like a picture painted a long time ago, and it horrified her to see the boy dragging the bellpull out of the wall and hanging on to it while a solemn peal sounded far away, muffled and sad, as though it rang at the bottom of the sea. . . .

She realized that her father was speaking to her. "I expect to find her very odd. You must not laugh and if your surroundings seem unusual you must not say so." Of course she would not say so, thought Mary, as she climbed out of the trap. Of course things would be unusual inside a picture. What did her father expect?

The door opened inwards very slightly. The boy had jumped into the trap and driven away and her father, his hand on her shoulder, was urging her gently forward. She hung back, then grabbing at her courage she pushed through with her father behind her. The door shut behind them and they were in a scented darkness. At least that was how it seemed to her at first as she stood on worn paving stones with her back to the door, and to the little man in a leather apron, a gardener perhaps, who had opened it and was now talking to her father. She took no notice of them for they did not seem to exist for her. She was alone in the world inside the picture. It had seemed dark but now the light was silver. The paving stones were those of a narrow paved passage with four delicate fluted pillars on each side. The roof was made of wooden beams holding the weight of a great wistaria vine that entirely covered them and hung down in curtains of scent and colour on either side. Beyond the leaves and flowers Mary was dimly aware of birds singing in a garden.

At the end of the passage a little old woman in a black dress, with snowy mob cap and apron, stood at an open door smiling and holding out her hand. Mary went to her and took her hand and passed with her into a dark stone-flagged hall where a silver tankard of lilies of the valley stood on an oak chest. The flowers and the polished silver gathered all the light to themselves and Mary gazed at them entranced, . . . and suddenly she was no longer an intruder in this world inside the picture. It was her own world. . . .

Then she was upstairs and the old maidservant was pouring water out of a brass jug into a basin patterned with honeysuckle, and washing her hands and face. The soft towel smelled sweet against her face and even when it momentarily covered her ears she could still hear the birds singing. . . . Then she was standing on a dark, uncarpeted staircase and the worn treads sank in the middle like the steps outside the green door. She walked down very slowly, carefully placing her feet on the hollowed wood that shaped itself like a curved hand to hold her safely. She was seated at a mahogany dining-table eating roast beef and Yorkshire pudding, and later apple tart and custard, while her father talked to the tall gaunt woman in the wide-skirted flowered dress who was sitting in the chair with the carved back at the head of the table. She did not look up from her plate, and she did not speak, for she was very frightened of Cousin Mary. She did not think her funny, she thought her terrible, with her light eyes bright as a bird's, her red hair piled untidily on the top of her head and her deep hoarse voice. Her hands were so thin they were like claws, covered with bright rings, and the long necklace she wore chimed when she moved. But the fear Mary felt then was nothing to what she felt later when the door of the small panelled parlour clicked shut behind her father, going out to smoke in the garden, and she was alone with Cousin Mary. But she was a brave child and she did not pull away when her wrist was nipped between a cold finger and thumb. She followed where she was led, over a mossy carpet scattered with roses, through the dim shadows of the room to where a sea-green light illumined a small round table with a plush cover, and set upon it a tall domed glass case.

"Look, Mary Namesake," said Cousin Mary and the child-like eagerness in her voice contrasted oddly with her deep voice. "Look there, my dear!"

At first Mary could see nothing, for the shadows of the green vine leaves in the little conservatory outside the window flickered over the glass case, but then Cousin Mary lifted it away and she saw the circles of velvet-covered wood, diminishing in height and held together by a central upright, making shelves for the display of a host of miniature treasures, fairy things of silver and gold, jade, pinchbeck, glass, ebony and ivory, all so small that only the eyes of a child could fully perceive their glory. But Cousin Mary's bright eyes were still as keen as Mary's. She knelt down, bringing herself to the same level as the child, and they were equals. Mary was no longer afraid of her. She had forgotten that she ever had been afraid. She had forgotten everything for time had stopped for her. She stood and gazed at the little things and it was the greatest moment of her life until now, more wonderful even than that moment when she saw the lilies in the silver tankard. Perhaps five minutes, perhaps a hundred years went by, and Cousin Mary gently touched a few things here and there with the tip of her finger, and talked to them softly, but Mary did not dare to touch. She scarcely dared to breathe. . . .

"An ivory coach, you see, Mary," whispered her cousin. "It's no bigger than a hazel nut but it's all there, the horses and the coachman and Queen Mab herself inside. Do you see her inside?"

Mary nodded speechlessly. She could see the fairy figure with the star in her hair, and the tiny delicate features of the child-like face. It did not occur to her that human fingers could possibly have made Queen Mab and her coach for she seemed timeless as Cousin Mary herself. They had always lived here in this world inside the picture and they always would.

"It's Dresden, my dear, this little tea-set. Dresden."

Mary had just been trying to think herself small, and smaller and smaller, so as to get tiny enough to sit beside Queen Mab in her coach, but she courteously allowed herself to get large again so as to gloat over the tea-set of frail white china patterned with forget-me-nots. The cups and saucers and plates and teapot looked as though they had been fashioned out of thin egg-shell. There were several of these tea-sets, of glass, china, gold and silver. There were birds and animals, a dwarf with a scarlet cap, candlesticks and lanterns, and telescopes with microscopic pictures that you could see when you held the telescope up to the light. There were wooden dolls no larger than Mary's little finger-nail, with chairs for them to sit on and a cradle for the wooden baby. There were so many things that Mary lost count of them. But it was Queen Mab and her coach which she loved best, and the smallest of the tea-sets, the one made of clear blue glass, airy as a blown soap-bubble. She yearned to possess these two and her eyes clung to them, yet when Cousin Mary said, "Would you like to have something for yourself, dear?" she shook her head. They would have no place in the London house, Queen Mab would die there and the tea-set dissolve at the first crash of a banging door. "It's noisy in London," she said. "There are no trees in our street, and the birds don't sing like they do here. They wouldn't like it."

"Perhaps not," said Cousin Mary. "No, I don't think they would. I've never wanted to give anything away before, except once when I wanted to give the dwarf to a little boy, but you're different. You're my namesake. You're Mary Lindsay like me. My dear, I want to tell you—"

But Mary never knew what her cousin wanted to tell her because the church clock struck four, the door opened and her father came in, followed by the old maidservant with the tea. Cousin Mary lifted the glass case back over her treasures and turning round said to Mary's father, "She has seen my little things." She spoke gravely, in awed tones, as though something tremendous had happened, but he only nodded pleasantly and standing with his back to the fire he began to chat about the weather, and he did not even glance at the little things. But Mary knew that he was wrong and Cousin Mary was right. Something very important had happened.

[Adapted from *The Scent of Water* (1963)]

Designs of the Heart

Escape for Jane

BASED ON A TRUE INCIDENT IN THE LIFE OF JANE AUSTEN

THE PARLOUR OF Steventon Parsonage was lit only by the firelight. It flickered and gleamed on the white-washed walls, staining their whiteness orange. "Sunset on snow," said Jane to herself, looking up for a moment from her writing. She was crouching close to the fire, so as to get its light on her pencil and paper, and she looked adorable. She had masses of dark hair piled on top of her head, dark, vivacious eyes, a firm chin, a laughing mouth and dimples. She was dressed in her best dress, white muslin with cherry coloured ribbons, because she was going to a ball in ten minutes' time.

She had completely forgotten the ball and was crushing her dress to smithereens. She was writing a novel called *Pride and Prejudice*, and for the time being nothing existed for her but the people in her story. They were moving before her eyes as she wrote like actors on a brilliantly lighted stage, and the real world and the people in it were as shadowy and dim as a crowded, darkened auditorium.

The parlour door was flung open, letting in what seemed a blinding light from the lamp in the hall, and Mrs. Austen, cloaked and furred, with her elder daughter Cassandra and her sailor sons Francis and Charles, all decked out for the ball, entered upon Jane. . . . Instantly the lights in the auditorium flamed out, the stage was darkened and the curtain, sliding down, hid that little group of breathing, living creatures from their creator. . . . She sighed and stirred a little, letting her pencil and paper fall on to her lap and rubbing her knuckles in her eyes.

"My dear Jane!" cried Mrs. Austen in horror. "Look at your dress!"

Most writers, disturbed in a creative moment, hurl their manuscript across the room, or burst into tears, or stamp or swear, or do anything unpleasant that occurs to them as likely to lay stress on their superiority to the common herd. But that was not Jane's way. She uncurled her long legs and rose to the full height of a tall, slender figure in one graceful movement. Then she stood, smiling ruefully, all her dimples showing and her eyes sparkling.

"I'm a bad girl," she said.

She had discovered long ago that if she blamed herself her admiring family immediately fell into paroxysms of admiration and affection. . . . They did so now. . . . Although she was making them late for the ball they uttered no word of complaint. Her mother shook out the crumpled folds of her dress, her sister tidied her curls and her brothers went racing upstairs to fetch her fan and her cloak and her handkerchief and her dancing sandals. Old Digweed, the coachman, strolling in from the coach outside, stood in the parlour door to admire her and Mr. Austen, issuing forth from his study to say good-bye to his family, kissed her three times instead of the regulation once.

"Now then, Digweed," said Mrs. Austen, hustling her offspring towards the coach. "We are going to Langford Manor. The young ladies are to spend a few days there but I and the young gentlemen will require to be driven back." She paused and eyed him sternly. "You hear me, Digweed? We shall require to be driven back, and you must therefore remain sober. If you upset me out of the coach into the ditch again, under the impression that I am a wheelbarrow full of rubbish for the bonfire, I shall be seriously displeased."

"Darn it, marm," grumbled Digweed. "'Twas a frosty night t'other night an' the roads like glass, so they was, an' not the Archangel Gabriel himself, as sober as an owl on a post, could 'ave prevented that there coach—"

"That will do, Digweed," said Mrs. Austen, and the coach door being shut upon them, they jolted off into the darkness.

Francis and Charles, home from the sea for Christmas, were in such hilarious spirits that Jane's unusual silence passed unnoticed.

She sat in her corner watching the hedges, shining whitely in the light from the coach lamps, pass by her like an unwinding ribbon and as she watched she thought hard. To-night was a turning-point in her life and she did not know in the least which way to turn. The preoccupation of her family with her appearance had not been caused only by their love for her. They knew, and she knew, that before the ball was over she would have been proposed to by Sir Benjamin Jamieson-Carroway, the squire of Langford Manor, and they very badly wanted her to say, "Yes, dear Benjamin."

Jane, too, with one part of herself, wanted to say, "Yes, dear Benjamin." She liked Benjamin. He was good and affectionate and easily led, and he was bullied by the formidable aunt who kept house for him and he was lonely and he loved her. She had known him since they were both children and she had always enjoyed protecting him and petting him and telling him what he ought to do. For Jane was very strong-minded and people who needed her help appealed to her far more than people who didn't.

And then she loved Benjamin's beautiful manor house and she loved every stick and stone and flower of this county of Hampshire in which they both lived. She could never bear to leave Hampshire and if she married Benjamin she would never be asked to leave it. She didn't really love him but yet she thought she would never be fonder of any man than she was of Benjamin. She did not ever expect to fall in love in the usual way for she had long ago discovered in herself a queer self-sufficiency. She did not seem to depend on the usual human relationships for her happiness, but yet at the same time she found great joy in them. Yes, she was sure that she could make a success of marriage with Benjamin.

That was one side of the question and it weighted the scales very heavily, but on the other side was that brilliantly lighted stage with the little figures moving about on it. If Jane were to marry she would not be able to give the whole of her heart, brain and soul to the writing of novels, and that was what, with the other part of her, she wanted to do. Of course she could not say that to anybody for they would have thought her mad. In the year 1797 literature was not really considered a suitable pursuit for young females, and ladies who so far forgot themselves as to put pen to paper usually had sufficiently good taste to refrain from publishing what they perpetrated.

But Jane wanted to publish what she perpetrated. She wanted to reform the English novel. She considered that it needed it. It was silly, she thought, to write books about haunted castles and ladies who died of love. The castles only made people dislike beautiful things like downy owls and the cry of the wind at midnight, and as for dying of love Jane didn't think it should be encouraged; what the love-sick needed was a smacking and some work to do. No, Jane wanted to represent the real world as worthy of attention. To love things as they were, she thought, was the way to be happy. Everyday life was perhaps hard, yet if novelists pointed out its funny side and its inherent beauty it would perhaps be easier. . . . But if she was going to do that she would have to give the business her whole attention.

She was still quite undecided as to which turning to take when the coach jolted up the drive of Langford Manor and stopped by the front door. It was flung open and Benjamin himself came hurrying out to meet them in a new blue coat, with his cravat too tight and his face shining with welcome.

"Jane, will you dance the minuet with me?" he whispered anxiously as he handed her out of the coach.

"I'll help," said Jane, and gripped his hand reassuringly.

Benjamin trying to dance the minuet always looked like a lost puppy trying to find itself and Jane was the only partner in the neighbourhood who was of the slightest use in the search.

Brackets of lighted candles hung all round the panelled hall, their twinkling flames reflected in the dark wood, and the music of the minuet, played by three violins and the harpsichord, seemed in its sweetness the expression of light in sound. The dancers, flowerlike in their slenderness, bowed and curtseyed and drifted and turned, slowly and very gracefully, as though the music were a spring wind that swayed them earthward and the candlelight sunshine that lifted them again. They did not talk at all for the minuet was the opening of the ball, a solemn ritual that would be followed later by more frivolous country dances when tongues would be loosed and restraint broken up.

Jane opened the ball with Benjamin and all eyes were upon her, for with her length of limb and slender grace she was the best dancer in the whole county. She meanwhile was entirely occupied in keeping Benjamin from losing himself. When they were together she whispered instructions and when they were parted she guided him with movements of her fingers. It was an unusually successful dance, and when Jane sank into her final curtsey she had the satisfaction of knowing that Benjamin had only once stepped backwards on top of the man behind him and had only led the wrong way twice.

"You were wonderful, Benjamin," she congratulated him.

But Benjamin, with the true modesty of all successful men, insisted that the credit was hers.

"I can't do without you, Jane," he whispered hoarsely.

She felt that the remark was ominous, and when he offered her his arm and inquired with increasing hoarseness if she would like to see the portrait of his great-grandfather in the next room she grew alarmed.

"But Benjamin," she protested, "I've seen it practically every day for the last twenty years. Don't you think you'd better take me back to mamma?"

"It's just been cleaned," whispered Benjamin, now so hoarse that he could hardly articulate, and led her firmly to the adjoining parlour.

They stood in silence, arm in arm, before the late Sir Montague Jamieson-Carroway.

"You wouldn't know he had been cleaned," said Jane. The occasion, she felt, was solemn, like in Church, and she hardly dared to raise her voice.

"No," said Benjamin. "But he has been. Shall we sit down?"

They sat down side by side on a settee and Benjamin, clearing his throat, thrust a forefinger inside his too tight cravat. Jane felt that her hour was upon her and clutched her hands nervously together on her lap, for she still did not know which way to take and a sudden overwhelming desire to giggle was almost robbing her of breath.

"Miss Austen," said Benjamin solemnly. "There is something that I wish to say to you. Be patient with me while I try and find words in which to—to—"

He paused, breathing heavily through the nose, and Jane prodded him gently as she had done in the nursery days when they shared the same governess and he forgot his piece.

"I cannot find words in which to express the admiration and esteem," she prompted softly, but he took the wind out of her sails by suddenly putting his arms round her and whispering against her curls, "Jane, I love you. You must marry me. You must."

Jane was done for. Had he proposed in the proper manner, leading up through graceful introductory remarks to the proposal, and then passing on to the peroration on one knee and the kissing of her hand, she would have had time to think, but this frontal attack sent all her defences flying. Before she realized what she was doing she was sitting on his knee, the future Lady Jamieson-Carroway of Langford Manor.

She spent a miserable evening, though she danced and laughed and curtseyed her way through it as though there was not a cloud in her sky. She had discovered before that though you may hover undecided for weeks between two courses the moment you make a decision this way or that you know within minutes whether you have decided right or wrong. . . . And she had decided wrong. . . . Her decision was unfair to Benjamin because she didn't really love him, and unfair to herself for the same reason, and above all unfair to the unborn children of her mind who depended on her to give them life. And all through the long evening, whenever she was with Benjamin, she felt a sense of suffocating imprisonment. She had not realized before how much she valued her independence but now that it was threatened she knew it was vital to her.

Towards the end of the evening someone asked her to sing. She didn't want to, for she didn't feel like singing, but she always sang country songs at the Langford balls and so she had to say yes. Yet when she sat down at the harpsichord the words and music that came to her were those of a song she had made up herself one wet day at home, and hardly knowing what she did she sang it.

> Nightingale, why do you wake
>   Lone in the night?
> Are you not sad in the falling dews,
>   The stars' cold light?

I have a song I must sing,
  A tale to tell,
Though I should die in the dark alone,
  Echo my knell.

Other birds sing in the sun,
  Blackbird and thrush.
Can you not join in the ecstasy
  Breaking dawn's hush?

Then is my song unheard,
  Lost in their praise,
Then is my passionate tale untold,
  Wasted my days.

Can a song hold jewelled truth,
  Gleaming yet pale?
Is life's sure answer to sullen death
  Held in a tale?

Wake when the moonlight sinks down,
  White as the snow.
Listen alone in the silent night,
  Then you will know.

When she had finished there was a pause of surprise, for this was not the merry sort of song that Jane Austen usually sang. Benjamin, leaning on the end of the harpsichord, looked at her with puzzled eyes. He thought it odd that she should sing him a song in praise of solitude.

Jane was glad when it was all over and she and Cassandra were shut up together in the big room with the four-poster that they were to share together.

They put on their dressing-gowns and settled themselves in front of the fire to curl their hair. Fair-haired pretty Cassandra was to be married in a few months to one Thomas and she was very distressed about her curls.

"Jane," she said, "my curls worry me. What am I to do when I am married to Thomas? I don't want Thomas to know I put my hair in curl papers, and yet if I don't put my hair in curl papers I shall look a fright and Thomas won't love me any more."

"This question of matrimony is extraordinarily difficult," said Jane, and sighed deeply.

Cassandra glanced up sharply. "Jane, darling, did he say anything?"

Jane got up, her hair unfinished and three curl papers sticking straight up on top of her head like a cock's comb, and crossing over to the little writing table at the foot of the bed, sat down, pulled a piece of paper towards her and dipped her pen in the ink.

"Yes," she said. "He asked me to be her ladyship and I said I would be her ladyship and now I'm writing to say I won't be her ladyship. . . . I can't say it to his face, I must write it."

"Jane!" cried Cassandra, her comb arrested in mid air.

"For a strong-minded woman who prides herself on never changing her mind," said Jane, "I consider that I have behaved badly."

"But why won't you have poor Benjamin?"

"Because I am going to have my dreams instead." She laid down her pen and put her hands behind her head, laughing. "They are lovely dreams, Cassandra, funny and true. They will be born of me and I will send them out into the world like pigeons from a dovecot. I shall never know how far they will fly but I do know that I must send them out. They are there in my heart and my brain, beating with their soft wings and crying to me to go free."

Cassandra tied her nightcap over her curl papers, took a run and a jump, scaled the side of the huge bed and landed among the pillows. Here she sat enthroned to scold Jane. She loved her dearly but she was very annoyed with her.

"You are being perfectly ridiculous, Jane! Fancy putting real things like Benjamin and his manor house second to unreal things like silly stories that you haven't even written yet."

"But what is reality?" asked Jane. "Is not reality more often the intangible than the tangible? Which is more worthy to be called real, the unborn symphony in the musician's brain or the spider that is just going to drop on your face?"

Cassandra screamed and disappeared from sight beneath the bedclothes while Jane seized the opportunity of quiet thus procured to finish her letter. She signed it and sealed it, and dropped a kiss on it so that it shouldn't hurt Benjamin too much, and then called to Cassandra, "Come out, darling, it's gone."

"Well, all I can say is," said Cassandra, reappearing, "that horrible spider is more real to me than any dull symphony in the brain of a tiresome man I shall never see; so your argument is disposed of."

"No, darling, because there *is* no spider. He is just a real idea existing in my mind."

Cassandra dropped crossly back on her pillows. "I wish you would not talk such nonsense, Jane. It all comes of Papa teaching you about the arguments of Socrates. Mamma always said it was a great mistake. ... And why in the world can't you marry Benjamin and write your stories, too?"

"Because the vicinity of Benjamin would be the death of any dreams. He never thought a clear thought or imagined a whimsical thing in his life. And then his wife would have no time for dreams. The hours that were not spent in ruling the household and the village with an iron hand would be entirely occupied in helping Benjamin scratch the pigs' backs. ... He is a companionable man and hates to work alone."

"I think you're quite mad, Jane," mourned Cassandra.

"I expect I am, darling," said Jane cheerfully. "All the nicest people are."

She returned to the fire and her curl papers—there were twenty of them by the time she had finished—and then she tied her nightcap over the finished work of art, blew out the candles and went to the window to pull back the curtains and look at the night.

She always slept with the curtains drawn back so that she could see the stars if she woke up in the night, and could exult with the birds at the first flush of the dawn. Cassandra, who always felt creepy in the moonlight and preferred having her sleep out to exulting with any birds, however melodious, found her habits very trying sometimes, but she loved Jane too much to say anything.

"Come along, Jane dear, do," she sighed. "You'll catch your death."

Jane lifted the skirts of her nightgown, took a run and a jump and landed on top of Cassandra. They cuddled down together in the great bed, completely disappearing from sight among the hills of pillows and the bulging feather mattress and the enormous quilt.

"It's a bit cold in this mountain range," said Jane. "They couldn't have left the warming-pan in for more than two minutes. Let's kick a bit, Cassandra, shall we?"

They kicked rhythmically until their circulation was restored and then Cassandra got drowsy. But not so Jane. Her mind, tormented by her treatment of Benjamin and alight with her ambition, was terribly active.

"Cassandra," she said, prodding her, "look at the lovely moon. Isn't it consoling to think of the moon shining down changelessly year after year on all our aspirations and bewilderments? I expect she thinks there's nothing remarkable in any of it. We blossom and wither and perish but nothing upsets the moon. She's so comforting."

"Why?" asked Cassandra crossly.

"Most of the changeless things, like love and justice, one cannot see and that makes them a little irritating sometimes, but the sun and the moon and mountains are the symbols of them and vouch for their existence."

"Yes, Jane," said Cassandra. "And now shall we go to sleep?"

"Symbolism fascinates me," said Jane, wide awake. "If you come to think of it everything in the world can be taken as the symbol of something else, and you can pass from one thing to another, mounting higher and higher, until at last you come to— what?"

"Jane," implored Cassandra, "couldn't you think about something that would make you feel sleepy? Couldn't you count sheep getting over a gate?"

"Those never-ending sheep are a symbol of eternity," said Jane brightly. "I suppose that is why one thinks of them when one wants to feel sleepy. Eternity is reached through death and the symbol of death is sleep."

"My dear Jane! Don't *think* about the sheep, *count* them."

"Very well, darling," said Jane meekly, and there was complete silence for a long time while she fixed her attention on white, leaping woolly backs.

"Cassandra," she said at last.

"Yes?"

"The gate has suddenly disappeared. What do I do now?"

"Stop talking for heaven's sake!" implored Cassandra, and turning over she flung herself down on the other side for another attempt at slumber.

"Cassandra," whispered Jane, "are you very angry with me? Please don't be angry. I can't help it about the gate."

"Darling," said Cassandra relenting.

"We will love each other till our lives' end, won't we?" said Jane. "How ever many husbands you have—consecutively, of course—they shall never come between us."

"No," said Cassandra sleepily. "Not how ever many."

"Good night, darling Cassandra."

"Good night, darling Jane."

Just as the dawn was breaking Cassandra was rudely awakened from a dream in which Thomas had been perfectly sweet about the curl papers and hadn't minded a bit. Jane was standing beside the bed shaking her and she saw to her astonishment that she was fully dressed.

"Get up, Cassandra," cried Jane. "I've been having the most dreadful dreams about Benjamin."

"I can't see that that's any reason for waking me up in the middle of lovely dreams about Thomas," complained Cassandra.

"Yes it is, because you've got to get up and dress and run away with me."

"What?"

"I said you've got to run away with me," said Jane, and pulled her sister out of bed.

"But we're staying here on a visit," objected Cassandra, swaying with sleep. "We've only just come."

"And now we're going," said Jane. "Wash your face, Cassandra, while I take your curl papers out."

While she hustled her sister into her clothes Jane talked.

"After the dreams I've had, Cassandra, if I see Benjamin again I shall marry him to a certainty. I dreamed that because I didn't marry him he danced the minuet backwards instead of forwards and fell over and died. And then I dreamed that because I didn't marry him he invested his money all wrong and something burst and he went to prison and died. And then I dreamed—but I can't go on, Cassandra, it was awful—and if I see Benjamin I'm sure to say 'yes' after all, so we must run away."

"But we all want you to say 'yes,'" mourned Cassandra. "Don't pull my stay laces so tight, I can't breathe."

"And there's another thing," said Jane, popping Cassandra's petticoat over her head. "One half of me, the least worthy half, would like to marry Benjamin and be 'your Ladyship,' and my least worthy half is always most active in the mornings. Don't you think, Cassandra, that when one comes down to breakfast, feeling empty and smelling coffee, that it is very hard to believe one has a soul? I know quite well that if I go down to breakfast in this house this morning that I shall decide to marry Benjamin again. So I am going to put it out of my power to betray my dreams by running away from temptation."

"But we shall meet the housemaid as we go down the stairs," objected Cassandra. "We might even meet Benjamin."

"We're not going down the stairs," said Jane, "we're going out of the window."

"Jane!"

"This room is so low. It's only a small drop to the top of the porch below and from there to the ground by way of the water-butt is only child's play."

"I daresay, but we're not children any more, we have skirts."

"We'll take them off if they incommode us."

Cassandra sighed despairingly. "Whatever will Mamma say?"

"We shall soon know," said Jane, with just a trace of gloom in her voice.

They were ready now, with their luggage packed ready to be fetched later and their bonnet strings tied under their chins. Jane picked up her letter from the table.

"Have you a large pin so that I can pin my letter to the pillow?"
she asked.

"Why the pillow?"

"My dear, when a woman is deserting a man she always pins
the fatal note to the pillow."

"Not the pillow, the pincushion."

"Are you sure it's the pincushion?" said Jane anxiously. "I am
behaving so very badly in the aggregate that I should like to be
correct in the little details."

"Of course it's the pincushion," said Cassandra. "You've only
to look in any novel to find it's the pincushion."

"Very well, then," said Jane, planting her note. "And now to
cross the Rubicon."

She threw her long legs over the windowsill, poised herself, and
with a sudden small scream disappeared. Cassandra, rushing to
the window, saw her on all fours on the top of the porch below.

"Jane, my dear, are you hurt?" she asked.

"Not in the least," said Jane. "It's quite easy once you let go."

Cassandra put her legs doubtfully over the window ledge and
spoke shakily. "What a glorious morning. So pure and fresh."

"You'll appreciate the beauties of nature far more when you're
down here with me, dearest," said Jane. "Just let go. I'll catch
you."

Cassandra averted her head. "I just can't do it, Jane."

Jane got to her feet and spoke in a sepulchral tone. "Do you not
realize what is at stake, my love? Do you not realize that our
smallest actions affect the course of history? If you, Cassandra
Austen, let go of that windowsill here and now I, Jane Austen,
shall escape from the grip of material things and all the pretty
pigeons in my mind will be set free. But if you insist on remaining
where you are I shall have to come back and join you, and what
then? I shall be imprisoned for life and all my dreams will die."

"You can go without me."

"And face Papa and Mamma alone? No, thank you. Think of
posterity, Cassandra. Think of the poor world if my pigeons never
fly out into it. This is a great moment, Cassandra, in the history of
the English novel."

Cassandra let go with a shriek and fell into Jane's arms. They collapsed together in a heap on top of the porch.

"There!" said Cassandra. "Now I've torn my best petticoat."

"Never mind, Cassandra," said Jane. "The English novel is saved."

[Taken from *White Wings* (1952)]

An Artist in Love

To BEN JUST now, the love of a woman meant more than anything had ever meant; except his painting, with which it was so inextricably confused that he could not put paint upon canvas without thinking of Zelle, or see Zelle without wanting to paint her just exactly as he was seeing her at the moment. The gallery of his mind was hung all round with portraits of Zelle in every attitude, mood and frock that she possessed. . . . He had only lately discovered the joys of portrait painting, for until now it had been the beauty of earth and of legend that had absorbed him. They had seemed one, even as now the thought of Zelle and the thought of painting were one. . . .

"It's odd how when you're in love it can all come to a focus in one person," he said to Zelle. Only he did not call her Zelle, which was her nickname, but by her own name of Heloise.

"What's all come to a focus in me?" asked Zelle. They were walking quickly, for Ben wanted to get to Brockis Island, his special place, and show it to her. . . . Sometimes the rough tweed of his coat touched her bare arm as they swung along under the trees, and she thrilled at the light touch, longing for Brockis Island and the kisses he would give her there. It was strange to be longing for a man's kisses, because for much of her hard young life she had been warding them off. But, then, Ben's odd, delicate, fastidious love-making was no more like other men's than he himself was like any other man she had known or imagined. No, that was not quite true, for in the worst of the bad days she had comforted herself with an imagined impossible lover not unlike Ben. The fantasy lover had been wonderful to look at, of course, which Ben was not, but he had been gentle as Ben was and he had loved in her some suffering thing, hidden in some place of deep peace within her, that had nothing to do with her being a woman, and nothing to do with those dark fires that lit up when men wanted her who were not gentle, and that made her so terrified both of herself and them.

"What do you mean, Ben?" she asked again.

"When I try to paint it isn't only the shape and colour that I like," said Ben, "it's the something that you don't see creating the shape and colour from within. And possessing it from without, too, like the invisible air that holds us. It's hard to explain. And why the dickens do I use such a milk-and-white word as 'like'? Worship would be better. 'With my body I thee worship', the man says in the marriage service. You seem all the beauty of the world that I worship, and the invisibility that makes it visible, focused in just one being whom I can love and serve mortally and immortally with all the powers of my body and my soul."

Zelle was not sure that she knew quite what he was talking about; and she was not sure that he was as sure as he thought he was. Compared to her he was a child in experience and knew things chiefly by intuition. She was the opposite. . . .

"I've never learned to see the 'idden beauty in things," she said humbly. "I've never even learned to see the outward beauty. I've never done anything but just scramble along. You'll 'ave to teach me. I 'ardly know even 'ow to be'ave."

The collapse of her h's, tumbling away so fast out of her lovely lilting speech—for she was French—was suddenly Ben's undoing, and he could scarcely wait for Brockis Island. They were nearly there. He took her hand and they ran along the sun-dappled path to the fallen tree-trunk that spanned the amber stream, and crossed it, quick and sure-footed as wild creatures of the woods.

They pushed their way through the loosestrife and bog-myrtle on the farther side, and came through the break in the rampart of thorn and crab-apple trees to the hidden depth of peace that lay inside. For that was how it appeared to Zelle as she looked round at the small perfect green lawn, roofed with branches, cool and fresh, fragrant with the scent of the bog-myrtle and silent with the silence of the deep woods in one of those midsummer pauses when the birds and the winds are still. This place had the same quiet as the deep peace within her where her suffering self lay hidden. Only just now that self did not suffer. There was nothing but joy to feel in this green shade that was so unbelievably lovely that it couldn't be true.

Then she was in Ben's arms and being kissed with a thoroughness not met before in Ben. Yet still there was the gentleness that she loved. She could yield herself to it, her whole body pliant in his arms, without any sense of fear, and laughing with amused delight.

"Why do you always laugh when I kiss you?" asked Ben, holding her away from him and looking down at her. He loved to see her like this, with the laughter banishing the taut look that was usually stretched like a mask across her face, and the sadness of her eyes that was so disquieting. There was nothing demanding in his eager look, only a delight in her and adoration of her that made her feel queen as well as woman, crowned as well as loved in this enchanted island that suddenly seemed her throne as well as her hiding-place. Outwardly she would seem to rule this man through their life together, but secretly he would be her refuge, though no one but themselves would know it. A love that is worth anything has its secrets, she thought, and they are fun to keep.

"I think I laugh because the unexpected is always some'ow funny," she said. "I thought it was only in dreams and story-books that men and women love this way. But, look, it 'as happened."

He picked her up and carried her to a fallen tree-trunk and sat beside her. Facing them was an old thorn-tree, and between the roots of it was the entrance to a badger's holt. They sat watching it, both of them oddly stirred. There was a home inside there, warm and intimate. "The brockis," said Ben softly. "Do you know him? He's stripey, with one of those fascinating *retroussé* noses, rather like yours."

"You Eliot men!" complained Zelle. "Do you always compare the women you love to wild animals? I've 'eard Monsieur Eliot telling Sally she looked like a lioness. That lovely Sally! It's an insult."

"Not at all," said Ben. "What's lovelier than a lioness? Or a brockis either. Black and white, he is. Beautiful markings. I'll tell you you look like a shy violet, if you'd rather, perjuring myself though I should be." He paused, and spoke again with a slight trace of exasperation. "Though maybe there's some truth in that simile, too. Heloise, why can't we have this out in the open? I hate holes and corners."

137

"Is this an 'ole and corner?" she flashed back at him. "This beautiful 'idden place?"

"No, no, no," he said, and swung round and took her face between his hands. He hated it when anger suddenly flamed up between them like this, as it did sometimes just when they were at their happiest. "There must always be the secret places of love, but why should love itself be secret? I want to tell the whole world that I love you, and you won't even let me tell Mother."

Least of all his mother, she thought. She might lose him that way. He adored his mother, and she had no illusions as to what Nadine would think of her as wife for her eldest son. Or his father, the General, either. The daughter of a murdered Jew and a secret service agent, who had been left alone to look after herself as best she could from her teens upwards, and was now nursery governess to their great-niece. Not at all the sort of daughter-in-law they would have hoped for or expected. These English might say they were democratic, and pride themselves upon their broad-minded tolerance, but she was shrewd, and she had noticed that the family pride of the English gentry died hard in them. At heart they were still deeply intolerant, whatever they might say, and Ben was not strong in character, and almost morbidly conscientious. He was vacillating and perpetually undecided as to which way duty lay. He had already, after torturing months of indecision, relegated his painting to the status of a hobby and chosen the Civil Service as a career, under pressure of what his parents told him was his duty. . . .

"Wait," she said, her flash of anger dying at the touch of his hands. "Never force things to 'appen, Ben, but wait and let what 'appens show you the way. I've learnt that. The spring comes slowly. The way will open out for us if we wait and are patient. You've never learnt patience, but I 'ave. Patience, *mon Dieu!* I've learnt it!"

He took her hands and held them tightly. The laughter had gone out of her face, and her eyes were sombre. He thought of the little that she had told him about her life. Her French mother had married against the wishes of her family, distinguished scientist though her husband was. But they had been very happy, and the little Heloise had been deeply loved by her parents and as loving.

The war had caught them on a visit to Poland, and her father had been murdered there, and his wife and daughter had seen him die. Somehow, through the chaos of those days, they had struggled back to France, and France had fallen. Penniless now, and filled with hatred, Heloise's mother had worked for the Maquis through much of the occupation. Then the Nazis had got her and she had died, and Heloise at seventeen years old had carried on where her mother had left off. She had hoped she would die, too, and so she had lived, as those do who hope for death. After the war she had done a great many things, and gradually life had come to seem to her not so bad after all, for she was healthy and still young. Then she had thought she would like to come to England to perfect her English. She was a clever girl, and she might have got a good teaching post, but she chose instead the care of little children. For she adored children. It was the child in Ben, so much in need of looking after, that had made her fall in love with him the moment she had set eyes on him. . . . But that she had not told him, and never would, for she was a supremely tactful woman. She was four years older than he was, and that, too, was a matter that she would never obtrude upon his attention.

"Forgive me," he said. "No, I'm not patient. There has been nothing to teach me patience. What have I ever suffered, compared with you? I'll go slow."

She pressed home her advantage. "You didn't go slow when you chose the F.O.," she said, and still holding his hands she bent forward and kissed him, so that he should not be too much hurt by what she said.

"I dithered for months," he said drearily.

"Dithered, yes; but that's not the same as going slow. Dithering is just going round in a circle, and giving in just the same at the end, as you might have done at the beginning. When you go slow you go patiently on, not round. And you get there, Ben. You get there."

"At the F.O. it won't take me too long to make a home for you," said Ben. "As a painter it might have been years before I'd been making enough to keep a wife."

"Do you think I want a comfortable 'ome at the cost of your integrity?" said Zella hotly. "I'd rather be very poor with you, or wait years before I married you, than commit murder."

"Murder?" asked Ben, shocked.

"Yes, murder," flashed Zelle. "If I kill the artist in you, demanding a comfortable 'ome, that will be murder. And if you kill 'im, just to please your parents or marry me quickly, that will be suicide. Oh yes, it will, Ben. That is, if you mean by integrity what I mean. What *do* you mean?"

"Constancy in service to my own vision," said Ben slowly. "My vision may not be the same as another man's, but if I serve his instead of mine I've lost my integrity. I see that that's a sort of murder. The vision and the man who might have served it are both killed. I don't know if I've quite understood what the Bible means by the sin against the Holy Ghost, but in my own mind I think of it as believing that I have seen the truth and believing that I know how I must serve it, and then deliberately doing the other thing. But I don't see what that's got to do with the F.O."

"Everything," said Zelle. "You've 'ad your vision; something within creating shape and colour, you said. You tried to explain to me, though I don't think I understood very well, and per'aps you did not either. But there is something you 'ave seen. Could you serve it as a Civil Servant?"

"Yes," said Ben obstinately. "All honest work serves it."

"Work isn't honest unless it's done by honest men," said Zelle. "Are you being honest when you deny you are a painter? For you do that when you were made one and won't be one. First you lie and then you kill."

"You're making the most enormous mountain out of a very small molehill," groaned Ben. "And I'm a rotten painter, anyway. If I were a genius it would be a different thing altogether."

"No, it wouldn't," said Zelle. "The question is, are you a painter or aren't you. Are you?"

"Yes," groaned Ben.

"Darling, don't let's talk about it any more," said Zelle. "I 'ad to say it once. I 'ad to tell you 'ow I feel. Now let's talk about the brockis."

[Adapted from *The Heart of the Family* (1953)]

A Pedlar's Pack

HE WAS TRAMPING from farm to farm over the Cornish cliffs, with his ash stick in his hand and his pack upon his back. It was a hundred years ago and the lonely farms still depended for needles and thread, ribbons and laces and golden ear-rings, china dogs and fancy knick-knacks, upon the tramping pedlars.

He was a tall, swarthy man, a Cornishman with Spanish blood in him, and an imperious temper that had descended through several generations from a gallant Hidalgo whose galleon had been wrecked upon the very rocks, covered with weeds of deepest crimson, that were now splintering quiet waves into creaming foam far below the Pedlar; foam that went flooding white as moonlight into a cave that hid there. His shoulders were bent beneath his pack and his body was as scarred by wind and weather as the twisted oak trees whose stubborn clumps stood between the farm-houses and the gales from the sea.

But there was no suggestion of storm in that evening's sunset. Horizontal lines of quiet grey clouds, with a rainbow threaded between them, lay over a sky green on the horizon and deepening through ultramarine to bright blue overhead. The valleys were already dark with the coming of night but on the high headlands the dying bracken burnt crimson in the last of the sun, and far out over the water the gulls' wings were touched with gold over a silver sea.

The Pedlar climbed a stone stile and sat himself down for a moment on a wall whose stones were bound together with turf and heather. It was early autumn and inland the sombre foliage of the trees in the valleys contrasted sharply with the buff-coloured, shorn harvest fields of the uplands. Two tall church towers, black against the sky, and a field of brilliant yellow mustard were accents in the landscape that somehow clutched at the heart.

There were no sounds to be heard but the crowing of a cock and the busy chirping of the crickets.

The Pedlar looked at it long and was satisfied. There was no softening of his grim face and had a stranger passed him at this moment he would have uttered no word, for the love of his country was too deep to find facile expression, but in his eyes there was a slight kindling and his step when he set out again had more spring in it.

He, like many Cornishmen and all Irishmen, had left his country as a young man in order to make money to return to it. He had not made money, for he was not of the type that makes money, but in his fiftieth year he had returned to it to tramp its lanes and cliffs as a ragamuffin pedlar; he who had once been of "the quality." Yet what matter, he thought, if he was what the world calls a failure? At least he had shouldered the pack of his life cheerily in a world full of gloomy pedlars, and the earth that would cover his body at last would be the earth of his own country.

The stony path that he followed dropped steeply and far below him he saw the lights of a fishing hamlet. It was time he looked about him for supper and bed, he thought, yet he had not the price of them in his pocket. The few coins he had earned that day he had flung, with the contemptuous curl of the lip that accompanied all his acts of charity, to a beggar by the wayside whose pitiable condition had touched him. If he was to sup and sleep that night he still had work to do in the town below, and he quickened his pace.

The path led him into a wooded valley where already it was night, so that he could hardly see the trees with their moss-grown branches or the steep banks of ferns that fell to the brawling stream so far below him.

And he did not see, until he was close upon it, the old grey manor house that stood among the trees, and its appearance startled him as though he had seen a ghost. The path was high up and the house was built on the wooded slope below, so that he looked down on its moss-grown roof, where in places the tiles had slipped and a gaping hole showed like a wound in a dead body.

... An empty house, he wondered? ... There was never yet a human being who could pass an empty house without looking in at the window, so leaving the path he fought his way down the side of the valley, through a thicket of brambles and ferns and moss, till he reached the front of the house where it faced the brawling stream.

Broken walls enclosed what had once been a terraced garden but now was a pitiful tangle of weeds and grass, and beyond it a small and lovely house was falling into ruin. He pushed open the rusty iron gate and made his way to it, the thorns of derelict rose trees scratching his face and trails of sweetbriar winding like tentacles round his feet. Everywhere the riotous white convolvulus scattered its moon-faces over the dusk and in the depth of the wood an owl was calling.

When he reached the house he found that trails of honeysuckle were flung across the door and a loathsome toad sat on the stone steps. "You shall not enter," they cried to him voicelessly. "No man shall enter here ever again."

He stepped to his right and looked through a broken window into the room within. Once it had been beautiful, with a fine carved mantelpiece and panelled walls, but now fungus obscured the carving and stains of damp disfigured the walls; while in the centre of the room the rats were dancing. ... A sickly odour of decay and death lay over the place and a sudden shuddering seized the Pedlar. ... In fear and loathing he fought his way back through the tangled garden and up the slope of the damp, unhealthy valley, until he reached again the path that was high up among the trees.

Here he could feel the breeze and there was no sense of fear. The scent of wet earth was in his nostrils and the smell of the sea.

The trees thinned and the path became a steep road rutted by the rivulets of water that rushed down it in wet weather. Below him he could see the grey roofs of whitewashed cottages and the orange glow of firelit windows.

The little town was a strange place and it was hard to believe that man had made it. The cottages that clung to the rocky cliff seemed themselves rocks, hollowed out by the action of the waves to form a shelter for sea creatures. The narrow, twisting streets that wound between them were like crevasses in the rock and the ruby lights in the windows were sea-anemones that clung to their sides.

The Pedlar made his way down to the harbour and sat on the sea wall. The boats had already gone out to their night's work and only a few old derelicts, barnacled and weather-worn, lay with their green sides reflected in the water and their masts bare.

The Pedlar, with his back to the sea and his face to the town, lit a foul black pipe and reflected. Up which of those streets should he climb, at which door should he knock? It pleased him to believe in destiny and he liked to ponder over such decisions, savouring to the full the romance of a man's life, with its turnings that lead he knows not where and its doors that open into rooms unknown.

To his right a street ended at the harbour wall with a flight of steps. An impatient street, it seemed, that could not wait to wind gently to the sea but must fall headlong. That pleased him for he too, when the sea called him, straight-way went to it. Shouldering his pack again and grasping his stick he climbed that street.

The houses that edged it were poor and mean, with outside staircases leading to doors where the paint was cracked and dim and windows where the light shone through panes that were broken. Not a very good choice for a hopeful merchant, thought the Pedlar grimly. Not through cracked doors does a man enter to do good business, and the suppers cooked behind broken windows are seldom succulent.

He climbed slowly, looking from side to side, but the finger of destiny did not seem to point more clearly to one house than another. It was not until he reached the top of the street that he paused, and then before an unlighted window.

Unlighted, that is, by firelight, but yet ablaze with colour, for it was filled with geraniums. Red geraniums, white geraniums and those brilliant salmon pink geraniums that are the pride of Cornwall.

"What now?" said the Pedlar. "Do they starve their bodies to feast their eyes or is this the house of a man whose purse can give him both bread and beauty?"

144

Curiosity was strong in him and he felt that he must know, so he climbed the outside steps and knocked three times.

"I have knocked three times in the Name of the Trinity," he said to the silent night, "and now I lift the latch in the Name of the God Who is One," and opening the door he walked in.

"God bless all here," he cried out in the geranium-scented darkness, but only a cricket answered him.

He struck a light and saw that the hearth was swept and the fire laid and the poor place neat and tidy. He struck another and saw that supper was laid for two and that the hands of the grandfather clock had stopped at midnight. He struck a third and lit the lamp that stood upon the oaken dresser.

Looking about him he saw that the room was swept and garnished, like that house out of which one devil was cast and to which eight devils returned. Though there were knives and forks and plates upon the table there was no food, and there were no pictures on the walls and no curtains at the windows. . . . Only that wealth of flowers.

It was always the habit of the Pedlar to follow the light of the whimsical fancies that flitted through his mind. Mad fancies, romantic fancies they might be, fancies that led him like a will-o-the-wisp into a bog at midnight. Yet what matter? Danger added a sauce to the dish of life and the fairest flowers grow away from the beaten track.

So now it seemed to him that a cold hearth cried out for the warmth of flames and a curtainless window for the privacy that makes a home. He lowered his pack from tired shoulders and he hung up his old hat on the nail behind the door. Kneeling before the hearth he kindled the driftwood that lay there, brooding over it until the flames that leapt up the chimney mocked at the geraniums in their brilliance.

Then opening his pack he took out of it a length of flowered cotton. He had seen it in a shop window when buying his needles and threads and laces and the red roses on it had taken his fancy. He had hoped to sell it for a good price to a farmer's lass, to make a dress to please her lover, but now he took it and ripped it in half as though it were of no more value than a cobweb. With pins in his mouth and his face grim with absorption he set to work to fasten it in place across the window, keeping it well behind the flowers so that autumn bloomed against the glow of a pictured summer.

Then he took from his pack a painted sailing ship set in a frame of sea-shells and hung it on a nail upon the wall. A poor, gaudy daub it was, showing a taller ship and larger waves than were possible even in the days when Spanish galleons dared the Channel, but it was a picture and therefore a mind's window. . . . For to the Pedlar a room in the leisured hours of evening should be curtained to the everyday world yet opened on far horizons. The fret of life's immediacy should be forgotten that the tide of eternal things may flow unhindered.

Then he looked about him. With a flame on the hearth and eternity upon the wall and privacy within the window there was yet no bread. Though man cannot live by bread alone yet assuredly he cannot live without it, thought the Pedlar, and he ransacked the cupboards. . . . The cricket protested but he took no notice.

Within them he found bread, sugar, butter, bacon, coffee, milk, two saucepans and a frying pan. To the Pedlar, who was more often hungry than not, this was riches indeed. "Wealth lives here," he said to himself, "but not happiness. This is a dwelling-place but not a home."

He filled the saucepans with milk and coffee and he cast butter into the frying pan with the lavish hand of a man who has not paid for it, and when it had melted away for very rapture he flung bacon and eggs into its golden sea. Merrily sizzled the bacon, joyously leapt the flames, and the prayer that rose to the Pedlar's lips was a heart-felt thanksgiving to the Giver of all good things.

When his meal was prepared he set it upon the table and bowed to the empty chair. It displeased his natural courtesy to be a hostless guest but there are things that will not brook waiting and a starving stomach is one of them.

Yet though he might be hungry the Pedlar was not un-fastidious. He tucked a darned handkerchief in at his neck to protect his patched old waistcoat and helped himself to only one egg at a time.

He had finished his third when a fumbling came at the door as a hand felt in the dark for an elusive latch. Laying his knife and fork neatly together, and wiping his mouth, he stepped to the door and flung it open with a kingly gesture. "Come in," he cried in his deep voice, "and welcome to you."

His rare and beautiful smile illumined his dark face, but the woman who stepped indignantly past his courteous figure had no answering smile. A crimson flush of anger marred her face and her dark eyes were dangerous. She flung her cloak aside as though it stifled her, strode to the hearth and faced him, her slender foot tapping impatiently and her head thrown back. If he was a king among men she was a queen, of the breed of Jezebel and Anne Boleyn. . . . He had only to look at her once to be reminded again of that swept and garnished room to which one devil had brought seven others.

"You will pardon this intrusion?" he said pleasantly, and again his smile challenged the cold white fury that had replaced her first crimson rage.

"That will depend upon the explanation that you are able to give me," she said.

She had had to fight hard with her anger, the muscles of her throat seeming to twist under the white skin, before the words would come, yet when they came they were clear and beautifully spoken. The Pedlar nodded his head once in brisk approval, for he liked a woman's voice to be a thing of beauty. He noted too, with further approval, how finely moulded were the nostrils that quivered in outrage as the scent of hot coffee and fried bacon assailed them.

"My coffee?" she queried.

"Excellent," he said. "Will you not join me in appreciation of it?"

He flung back his head and laughed, showing the white teeth that were still as even and strong as when he was a young man. Then his eyes dropped to her irritably tapping foot and his face changed. "Sit down," he commanded sharply, "while I take your shoes off. Where have you been that your feet should be soaking wet?"

It may be that his laugh disarmed her, or perhaps his abrupt command, a novelty to one who was never commanded, was not without effect, or perhaps she was just tired; in any case her rage seemed to fall from her and she dropped back into the chair by the hearth with a suddenness that startled him. . . . It was almost as though she were disintegrating.

Her shoes and the hem of her long green gown were soaked with sea water, and a coil of seaweed of deepest crimson was wound round her left instep. There was a mocking smile on her face as she stretched out her feet towards him. . . . She was wondering, perhaps, what he would do. . . . But embarrassment never troubled the Pedlar and he had never yet been known to treat any situation unromantically.

Stepping to his pack he took from it a spotted crimson kerchief, such as he sold to young girls to tie over their curls when they went about their business in dairy or stillroom, and a pair of green velvet slippers embroidered in crystal beads. Then kneeling before her, as though she were indeed a queen, he took off her shoes and rubbed her feet and her bare ankles dry with the kerchief. Then he slipped on the slippers, that he had had for long in his pack because they were too dainty and too slender to hold the bone and muscle of farm feet, and they fitted her as though they had been made to measure. . . . Her feet and her ankles, he noticed, were cold and white like ivory and by the fine bones of them he judged that the blood that ran in her veins was not lowly.

"And now," he said, "will you share my meal?"

He held out his wrist towards her with an air, a bony wrist protruding from the frayed cuff of a shabby coat, but as she laid her hand upon it and suffered him to lead her to the table she thought for a moment that fine linen surrounded it and there was a diamond ring upon his hand. . . . So successfully can a fine gesture create the illusion of fine haberdashery that she wondered that those with histrionic talent should ever put themselves to the trouble of dressing well.

He poured out her coffee and fried fresh bacon and eggs, and then they sat one on each side of the table and ate with daintiness but deep absorption, for both were hungry. The Pedlar, who had taken the keen edge off his appetite before she came in, was finished first. With his chin in his hand he studied her.

She was forty years old, he thought, for there were lines round her fine eyes and streaks of grey in her dark hair, but her tall figure was still slim and graceful and the lines of her firmly moulded mouth and chin were the clear lines of youth. Her long green gown was severe and plain; too plain, he thought, for the adornment of such beauty.

Opening his pack once more he took from it a necklace of polished Cornish stones, of that peculiar shade of green that is seen in the curve of a wave when the skies are grey. Clasping it round her neck he noticed that the lobes of her dainty ears were pierced. . . . So she had known, once, what it was like to wear fine jewels. . . . Going back to his pack for the last time he took out a pair of golden ear-rings shaped like sea-shells and with gentle fingers hung them in her ears.

She made no comment, only raising her eyebrows ironically as she went on placidly eating. Though events could still rouse her anger they could never, now, surprise her.

When she had finished her meal she wiped her fingers daintily on her handkerchief and spoke. "You have paid for your meal, sir, with a fine pair of shoes, but the gift of a green necklace and golden ear-rings has won for you something more."

Getting up she crossed to the grandfather clock that had stopped at midnight and lifted it aside. . . . So great was her strength that the burden seemed nothing to her. . . . Behind it was a little cupboard in the wall and this she unlocked with a key that hung round her neck, taking from it a black cobwebbed bottle and two crystal glasses most exquisitely shaped.

"Ah!" said the Pedlar with a long-drawn sigh of contentment. "You are right. So perfect a meal merits that conclusion."

"Draw your chair to the fire, sir," she said. "Lean back and watch the flames. Such liquor as I have here should be drunk by a man who is warm and dreaming, leisured and reverent, for there are flames and sunshine in it, stories and romance, and a man has died to bring it to you."

She sat opposite to him and she placed the bottle and beautiful glasses on a stool between them. He noticed that before she opened the bottle she made no attempt to remove the cobwebs and dirt that covered it.

"No," she said, answering his unspoken thought. "It seems to me that they cover a stain of blood."

He thought there was a flicker of madness in her eyes and there came over him that same shuddering and distaste that had seized him when he looked through the broken window of the empty house.

It was gone in a moment, as the firelight turned to molten gold the liquid that was tinkling slowly, drop by precious drop into the crystal glasses.

When they were full to the brim the man and the woman raised them and touched them softly together. Her hand, he noticed, was steady, though her face was white as death.

"Why," he asked, "do you open for me this drink that was brought you long ago by a man who is dead?"

"I do not know," she said, "I do not know."

He lay back in his chair and watched the flames and sipped the rare old wine, then he raised his eyes and gave her a curious look. Flames and sunshine were in it, stories and romance, and such drink, he knew, did not reach a hidden cupboard in a Cornish cottage by means that were lawful. . . . She met his look and smiled a little.

"I am leisured and reverent," he told her. "Warm and dreaming."

In the dreams that he dreamed with his eyes on the fire, six things were clearest in the flames; great weed-covered rocks where the creaming foam went flooding white as moonlight into a cave that hid there, an empty house in a wooded valley, a woman's feet wet with the sea, an uncurtained window, a clock that had stopped at midnight and a table laid for two.

She too was dreaming dreams as the hot embers fell into pictures and the brandy melted her misery, and each as they dreamed spoke to the other, gently and quietly, as man and wife who have been one for long.

"As I passed from the cliffs to the town," he said, "I passed through a wooded valley. Who lived in that empty house with the broken roof and the tangled garden?"

"Years ago," she said, "a man lived there who was proud as the devil and as wicked. He was of good birth, and had had great wealth, but twenty years ago there was little left of it but his only daughter and his ambitions for her."

"Were they not to her mind, these ambitions of his?"

"They should have been, perhaps, but she was proud, as proud as he was, and she would not marry tamely at his bidding. Instead, she lost her heart with passion to a man who lived in this cottage, a man dark and imperious as you are, who earned his living no one knew how."

"Perhaps," said the Pedlar, sipping his wine, "they did know how, but they stopped their ears when his step went by at midnight and closed their eyes to his shadow on the blind."

"So she went with her lover," murmured the woman, "and up in the house in the valley the man she was to have married fought a duel with her father, and the old man died. No one has lived in that house since he was carried out feet foremost, and no one will, for the country people think that his evil clings to it for ever."

"And she, who had worn silks and jewels proudly, was happy in this cottage?"

"She was happy, for the devil of her pride was cast out by the man who loved her."

"Though I am a Cornishman born and bred," said the Pedlar, "I do not come from this part of Cornwall; yet years ago as a boy I came here."

"Why?" she asked.

"To visit a reef of rocks, covered with weeds of deepest crimson, where even on quiet days the waves cream into foam. There a Spanish galleon was once wrecked and the founder of my family, so tradition tells me, was the one man saved. As a romantic youngster I climbed down to those rocks, a perilous climb it was, and found there a cave where the foam came flooding white as moonlight, but where a skilful and courageous man could have made his way into the hidden fastnesses. . . . A smugglers' cave, I thought. . . . A wonderful place to hide brandy and tobacco and all things contraband."

"A wonderful place," she agreed. "Its hidden fastnesses can be reached only by those who know the way."

"You know the way," he said, "and you go there often, even

though forbidden things are no longer stored there. You go as a woman goes to a tomb, to mourn over the dead. You remember always a night when a secret was discovered and a man was caught in that cave as a beast is caught in a trap. You remember a fight that was fought between law and outlaw, and a shot that was fired at random, and a man's blood that stained the creaming foam. When you return to your home at evening your feet are wet with the sea and the weed that grows over those treacherous rocks is coiled around your instep."

"Your eyes," she said, "are very clear to read a hidden story."

"Not hidden," he said. "It was written clearly in sparkling wine, and the wet hem of a woman's dress and a coil of crimson seaweed twisted around her instep."

"What else did you read?" she asked him.

"I read how on that night of the fight between law and outlaw a woman prepared supper for two in a flower-decked room. Then she watched at an uncurtained window for her lover, watched for the sight of his tall form moving through the evening shadows and listened for the sound of his feet on the cobbled street. Hour after hour she watched and when midnight struck from the church clock he returned to her, carried on a shutter and covered with a cloak."

"Yes?" she said.

"And I read that something twisted in that woman's mind, so that always her table is set for two and her window uncurtained, and the clock that stopped at midnight is for ever unwound."

"Yes?" she said.

"And after that day there was in the woman's mind and heart and home an emptiness more terrible than death, an emptiness that invited."

"Invited?"

"Invited back again that devil of pride that the man she loved had cast out. And so he returned, that devil, with seven others; loneliness, fury, hate, despair, self-pity, bitterness and blasphemy."

"Blasphemy?"

"You have no God."

The wine in his glass was finished and he rose to go.

"It is late," she said. "Will you not stay?"

152

"Have you no care for your reputation?" he asked her.

"Have you not heard my reputation? It is that of a woman both mad and bad."

"A lie," he said. "And it is not in my mind to give colour to it." He took his old hat from the nail on the door and bowed to her.

"Where will you sleep?" she asked him.

"A warm corner between two rocks or the leeward side of a haystack will do very well for a tramping pedlar," he told her.

"And will you come back?"

"In the morning I will come back and knock at your door. If you do not answer I will go away to the world's end but if you do answer I will come in to you till death shall part us."

He bowed again and she swept him a curtsey, her long green gown caressing the floor like a wave.

In the morning she had the fire alight and the parlour neat and tidy. The curtains at the window had made it homelike and on the wall the gallant ship on the sea of eternity gave to her restricted, tortured mind a lovely liberty.

Through the geraniums at her window she saw a tall figure moving through the shadows of the early morning, heard the sound of his step on the cobbled street and his hand at the door.

"I knock three times," he said, "in the Name of the Trinity."

"Lift the latch," she answered, "in the Name of the God Who is One."

[Taken from *White Wings* (1952)]

Patchwork of Portraits

The Man Who Loved Clocks

THE CANDLE FLAME burned behind the glass globe of water, its light flooding over Isaac Peabody's hands as he sat at work on a high stool before his littered work-table. Now and then he glanced up at it over his crooked steel-rimmed spectacles and thought how beautiful it was. The heart of the flame was iris-coloured with a veining of deep blue spread like a peacock's tail against the crocus and gold that gave the light. He had oil lamps in the shop and workshop but lamplight was not as beautiful as his candle flame behind the globe of water, and for work requiring great precision its light was not actually quite so good. And he liked to feel that through the centuries men of his trade, clockmakers, watch-makers, goldsmiths and silversmiths, had worked just as he was working now, in their workshops after the day's business was over, alone and quiet, the same diffused light bathing their hands and the delicate and fragile thing they worked upon. It banished loneliness to think of those others, and he was not so afraid of the shapeless darkness that lay beyond the circle of light. He did not like shapelessness. One of his worst nightmares was the one when he himself became shapeless and ran like liquid mud into the dark.

. . . He looked safe enough tonight in his halo of warm light. He was a round-shouldered little man with large feet and a great domed and wrinkled forehead, the forehead of a profound thinker. Yet actually he thought very little about anything except clocks and watches, and about them he not so much thought as burned. But he could feel upon a variety of subjects, and perhaps it was the intensity of his feeling that had furrowed his forehead, lined his brown parchment face and whitened the straggling beard that hid his receding chin. His eyes were very blue beneath their shaggy eyebrows and chronic indigestion had crimsoned the tip of his button nose. His hands were red, shiny and knobbly, but steady and deft. He dressed in the style of twenty years ago, the style of the eighteen-fifties, because the clothes he had had then were not yet what he called worn out. . . . His soft childish mouth was sucked in with concentration except when now and then he pouted his lips and there emerged from them a thin piping whistle.

He was happy tonight for one of his good times was on the way. Everything he did today, anything he saw or handled, had shape as though the sun was rising behind it. Presently it would happen to him, the warmth and glow of self-forgetfulness, and after that for a few moments or a few days he would be safe.

He had finished. The Dean's watch was now once more repaired and he knew he could not have made a better job of it. He held it open in the palm of his hand and gazed at it with veneration, his jeweller's eyepiece in his eye. It was inscribed "George Graham fecit, 1712". At that date Graham had been at the height of his powers. The inscription took Isaac back to the old bow-windowed shop in Fleet Street, next door to the Duke of Marlborough's Head tavern, which had been a place of pilgrimage for him when as a lad he had served his apprenticeship in Clerkenwell. Graham had worked in that shop, and lived and died in the humble rooms above it. Charles II's horologist, Thomas Tompion, whom men called the father of English clockmaking, had been Graham's uncle. Both men had been masters of the Clockmakers' Company and they had been buried in the same tomb in Westminster Abbey. Whenever he held the Dean's watch in his hands Isaac remembered that George Graham's hands had also held it, and that perhaps Tompion in old age had looked upon his nephew's handiwork and commended it.

For it was not only a beautiful watch but an uncommon one. It had a jewelled watchcock of unusual design, showing a man carrying a burden on his shoulders. . . . The pillars were of plain cylindrical form, as in most of Graham's watches. . . . It had a fine enamelled dial with a wreath of flowers within the hour ring. The outer case was of plain gold with the monogram A.A. engraved upon one side, and upon the other a Latin motto encircling the crest of a mailed hand holding a sword.

Isaac laid the Dean's watch down on his work-bench, amongst

the others he had finished repairing today, and opening a drawer took out an envelope full of watch papers neatly inscribed in his fine copperplate handwriting. The majority of horologists no longer used these but Isaac was attached to the old customs and liked to preserve them. In the previous century nearly every watch had had its watch pad or paper inserted in the outer case, either a circular piece of velvet or muslin delicately embroidered with the initials of the owner, or else the portrait of the giver, or a piece of paper inscribed with a motto or rhyme. Isaac had collected and written out many of these rhymes, and he would always slip a watch paper into the outer cases of the watches of the humbler folk, for their amusement and delight. He did not dare to do so with his aristocratic customers for he feared they would think him presumptuous. He shook out the papers and picked out one here, one there. . . . He slipped them into their various cases and then wrapped the Dean's watch in wadding and laid it away in a stout little box. Tears were in his eyes for he would not see it again until the Dean once more overwound it or dropped it. His fear of the terrible Dean was always slightly tempered by anger, because he took insufficient care of his watch, and then again by gratitude because but for the Dean's carelessness he would never have the lovely thing in his hands at all, for its mechanism was faultless. Because of this anger and gratitude he possibly had a warmer feeling for the Dean than most people in his Cathedral city.

Isaac took his own watch from his pocket and looked at it. It was a severely plain silver timepiece with tortoiseshell pair cases. He had made it for himself years ago. It said three minutes to eight and Isaac was dismayed, for it was later than he had realized and if he did not hurry he would be late for supper and incur his sister's displeasure. Yet the dismay quickly passed for today nothing had power to disturb him for long. He waited, his watch in his hand, for in a moment or two the city clocks would strike the hour and he liked to correct their timekeeping by his own faultless watch. It was quiet in the workshop, no sound but the rustle of a mouse behind the wainscot. It was a frosty October night of moon and stars and there was no wind. The city was still. There was no rattle of cab-wheels over the cobbles, no footsteps ringing on the pavement, for everyone was at home having supper. Isaac was aware of all the lamplit rooms in the crooked houses, little and big, that climbed upon each other's shoulders up the hill to the plateau at the top where the Cathedral towered, looking out over the frozen plain to the eastern sea. Another night he would have shivered, remembering the plain and the sea, but tonight he remembered only the warm rooms and the faces of men and women bent over their bowls of steaming soup, and the children already asleep in their beds. He felt for them all a profound love, and he glowed. The moment of his loving was in the world of time merely sixty seconds ticked out by his watch, but in another dimension it was an arc of light encircling the city and leaving not one heart within it untouched by blessedness. Then the clocks began to strike, and the light of the ugly little man's moment of self-forgetfulness was drawn back again into the deep warmth within him. And he understood nothing of what had happened to him, only that now, for a little while, for a few moments or a few days, he would be happy and feel safe.

The Cathedral clock, Michael, started to strike first, in no hurry to precede the others yet arrogantly determined upon pre-eminence. Its great bell boomed among the stars, and the reverberations of its thunder passed over the city towards the plain and the sea. Not until the last echo had died away was the city aware that little Saint Nicholas at the North Gate had been striking for some time. Only two of his light sweet notes were heard, but little Saint Nicholas was dead on time. Saint Peter in the market place waited for Nicholas to finish and then coughed apologetically, because he knew that his deep-toned bell was slightly cracked and he himself half a minute late. Saint Matthew at the South Gate struck a quick merry chime and did not care if he was late or not. Last of all Isaac's clocks in the shop all struck the hour, ending with the cuckoo clock. He kept them all a little slow so that he could enjoy their voices after the clocks of the city had fallen silent. Having refereed them all in past the tape he put away his own timepiece and rose slowly to his feet to set about the ritual of the Friday night shutting up of the shop. . . .

As he stumped up the street, he began to whistle one of his tunes, for the city about him was magical. His repertoire of tunes was small, all of them variations of a striking clock. He went through them one after the other almost without cessation when he was happy, driving his sister Emma almost crazy. In spite of the sharp incline he chimed twelve o'clock in every possible way all the way up Cockspur Street, his eyes on the crown of frosted stars above the Rollo tower of the Cathedral. Isaac did not like the Cathedral. It frightened him and he had never been inside it. Yet he always had to look at it. Everyone had to.

At the top of Cockspur Street, that was so steep that all the little bow-windowed shops had short flights of steps leading up to their front doors, Isaac turned right and was in the market place. . . . Just beyond Joshua Appleby's bookshop he turned sharply to the left and climbed a flight of steps between two high garden walls, a short cut to Angel Lane where he and Emma lived. It was a steep twisting cobbled lane bordered on each side by very old houses and crossed at its upper end by Worship Street, which curved about the great old wall which encircled the high plateau where the Cathedral towered, with the houses of the Close clustered about it. . . .

Isaac's little house was nearly at the top of the lane but before he turned to it he glanced eastward, and then stood spellbound by what he saw. Across Worship Street he could see the archway that led into the Close, the Porta, flanked by two small towers, cavernously black against the brilliance of the moonlit wall. Beyond and above it was a darkness of motionless trees, the great elms and lime trees of the Close that rose even higher than the wall. Beyond and above that again were the three towers of the Cathedral, the Phillippa and Jocelyn towers to the right and left and the central tower, the Rollo, soaring above them into the starlit sky with a strength and splendour that was more awful in moonlight than at any other time. Like the moon herself dragging at great waters the Rollo tower in moonlight compelled without mercy.

And the mailed figure above the clock face in the tower also compelled; above all he compelled a clockmaker for he was the finest Jaccomarchiadus in England. Like a fly crawling up a wall Isaac crawled up Angel Lane towards him, scuttled across Worship Street, cowered beneath the Porta, got himself somehow across the moonlit expanse of the Cathedral green and then slowly mounted the flight of worn stone steps that led to the west door within the dark Porch of the Angels. At the top he stopped and looked up at the Rollo tower, trembling. Then suddenly his trembling ceased for he was looking at the clock. He forgot his fear of the Cathedral, he forgot where he was, he forgot everything except the clock. He saw it from a distance every time he delivered watches in the Close but because of his fear of the Cathedral he was close to it only when, as tonight, he had been compelled. It was a Peter Lightfoot clock, less elaborate than Lightfoot's Glastonbury clock which had later been removed to Wells Cathedral, but in Isaac's opinion far more impressive. The Jaccomarchiadus stood high in an alcove in the tower, not like most Jacks an anonymous figure but Michael the Archangel. He was life size and stood upright with spread wings, his stern face gazing out across the fen country to where the far straight line of the horizon met the downward sweep of the great sky. Beneath his feet was the slain dragon, and his right foot rested on its crushed head. One mailed fist gripped the hilt of his sword, the other was raised ready to strike the bell that hung beside him. His stance was magnificent. Had he been a man it would have seemed defiant, but the great wings changed the defiance to the supreme certainty and confidence of the angelic breed. Below him, let into the wall, was a simple large dial with an hour hand only. Within the Cathedral Isaac had been told there was a second clock with above it a platform where Michael on horseback fought with the dragon at each hour and conquered him. But not even his longing to see this smaller Michael could drag Isaac inside the terrible Cathedral. No one could understand his fear. He could not entirely understand it himself. Yet every now and then, in spite of it, Michael compelled him to come and stand as he was standing now and look up at the clock, and then to turn and look out over the city from the central hub and peak of its history and glory. . . .

A tremendous music broke out over Isaac's head, and for a moment he was startled nearly out of his wits, for standing looking out over the city his mind had gone back to other years. Then a thrill of awe went through him. He did not look up, though he was vividly aware of the mailed fist striking the great bell and the stern face of the Archangel, but remained looking out over the past. Nine times the great bell boomed out, the sound rolling over Isaac's head and away over the city to the fens. Nine o'clock, the hour of the old curfew. Then far down below him he heard the homely church clocks striking. In all the houses of the city other little clocks were striking too though he could not hear them. Then there was silence, deep and profound, and suddenly he was terrified. It seemed to him that time was opening at his feet and that he stood looking down into an abyss of nothingness. Behind him the Cathedral soared like a towering black wave that would presently crash down on him and knock him into the abyss. Unable to move he stood there sweating with terror, as helpless and hopeless as in those nightmares that visited him during his bad times. But this was not one of his bad times, it was a good time. His mind suddenly gripped that. He remembered what had happened an hour ago and the memory was like a cry for help. Again and again he cried for help and slowly the memory of love became love, welling up from the depths of him and quietly enveloping himself and the city, time and the abyss, all that was. He was set free.

[Adapted from *The Dean's Watch* (1960)]

Miss Montague

Miss Montague sat apparently idle, her hands caressing the cat in her lap. Beyond the west window, behind the steep old roofs of Worship Street, the last of a fiery sunset was burning itself out. Through the east window she could see through the branches of the elm trees the west front and the three great towers glowing with reflected light, so that it seemed as though the whole Cathedral was built of rosy stone. Evensong was over and everyone was having tea. There was no sound but the ticking of her clocks and the cawing of the rooks in the elms. Motionless in her chair Miss Montague left her room and went up and down the streets of the city, seeing the remembered pattern of its roofs against the sky, the leap of the Cathedral towers seen now from one street and now from another, knowing as she turned each corner exactly what she would see, for she had the city by heart. She went out of the South Gate and down into the fen, and saw the great flaming sky reflected in the water. She told over the names of the villages on their hills as though they were a string of jewels, and came back into the city again and found that the lamplighter was going his rounds and the muffin man was ringing his bell. Lamps and candles were being lit in the houses now and she looked in through the windows and saw the children having their tea, but nobody noticed her. If anyone at this moment was thinking of her it was as a very old woman who never left her house except to go to the Cathedral in her bath-chair when she was well enough, and perhaps they pitied her. They did not know how vivid are the memories of the old and that only the young are house bound when they can't go out. Her memories ranged back over more than eighty years and covered a long span of the life of the city, and the birth and life and death of many men and women all of whom had been and were her friends. She did not forget a single one of them and now that she was so old she did not distinguish very clearly between those who were what the world calls dead and those who still lived there. No one had ever been so blessed with friends as herself. It astonished her. But then her whole life astonished her and caused her considerable amusement as she looked back upon it.

She had been born in this house. Her grandfather had been a famous judge and in his day Fountains had been only the holiday home of the Montague family, but her father, lacking the ambition possessed by nearly all the Montagues and gaining a rich wife, had retired early from the army and had lived for most of his married life at Fountains. His daughter Mary had come fourth in his family of six children, all of them attractive except herself. She had been from the beginning a plain little thing, and when a brother in a fit of temper pushed her down the tower stairs and she broke her leg the accident did not improve her looks. The leg, unskilfully set, mended badly and afterwards was shorter than the other. She had hurt her back also in the fall, and it caused her much suffering, but of this she never spoke after she had been told it was only growing pains. In a family of six aches and pains were not much noticed, least of all in the least noticeable of the children. And so she grew up stunted in her growth and slightly lame. She was shy and never had much to say for herself, and no one could have guessed, seeing the little girl sitting like a mouse in the corner with her kitten, that the ambition and the adventurous spirit that had made the later generations of Montagues such a power in the land was more alive in her than in any of the other children.

Through her early years she lived withdrawn from the others and their rowdy games, in which she could not join, happy in a fantasy world of her own. As soon as she could escape from lessons and the sewing of her sampler she would climb the tower stairs to the little room at the top, called Blanche's bower because it was said that it had been beloved of the duchess Blanche, who had occupied it centuries ago, and here she would sit in the window seat, wrapped in a shawl, with the cat in her arms, looking out over the roofs of the city to the fens and the sea, and dream of the great things she would do. She would be an explorer and discover unknown lands, and be adored by the natives there. She would be another Elizabeth Fry and her life would be written and she would be the friend of kings and queens and everyone would love her. She would marry an ambassador and live in fabulous Russia and have twelve beautiful children who would worship the ground she trod on. She would be a great actress like Sarah Siddons and every man who saw her would fall in love with her. There was no end to the entrancing careers that she mapped out for herself, and in all of them her starved longing for love was satisfied up to the hilt.

Her awakening in adolescence was sudden and terrible. Her eldest sister Laura was to be married. It was the first wedding in the family and was to take place in the Cathedral and be a great social occasion. It never occurred to Mary that she would not be Laura's bridesmaid with the other sisters. She was only a little lame and she could stand for quite a time when she had to. Yet the shock of being excluded was not so great as the shock of finding that in all the excitement of the wedding preparations no one, least of all her pretty careless mother, seemed to think it necessary to explain to her why she was left out. She realized that they had never thought that she would expect to be a bridesmaid. Towards the end of the wedding reception her back was hurting her so much that she could hardly bear it. She crept away, no one seeing her, grabbed the cat and went up to Blanche's bower and sat on the window seat wrapped in her shawl, for although it was a warm spring day she was cold. She heard, as from a great distance, the joyous turmoil down below, and presently she saw them come out into Worship Street to watch with the chief bridesmaid, her second sister, as the bride and groom drove away for the honeymoon. They were all there, her father and mother, the two brilliant brothers and the pretty younger sister who was already taller than she. Then full realization came to her. These brothers and sisters would do the kind of things of which she had dreamed, but she herself would never do them because the Mary Montague of her dreams was not the Mary Montague of the actual world.

She was two people but until now only one had been really known to her, and she did not want to know the other. Characteristically she did not stay for long where she was, waiting for someone to come and find her in the gloaming and offer her sympathy, but as soon as she was physically rested went downstairs to forestall it, but no one had missed her.

She had humour and common sense and she soon knew what she must do. She must have done with her dream world, laugh at the ridiculous Mary who had lived in it and get to know the Mary whom she did not want to know, find out what she was like and what her prospects were. It sounded an easy programme but she found it a gruelling one. The fantasy world, she discovered, has tentacles like an octopus and cannot be escaped from without mortal combat, and when at last her strong will had won the battle it seemed as though she was living in a vacuum, so little had the real world to offer the shy frustrated unattractive girl who was the Mary she must live with until she died. But free of the tentacles she was able now to sum up the situation with accuracy. She would not marry and being a gentlewoman no other career was open to her. She was not gifted in any way and she would never be strong and probably never free from pain. She was not a favourite with either of her parents, both of whom were vaguely ashamed of having produced so unattractive a child, and yet she was the one who would have to stay at home with them. And there was nothing to do at home. The prospect was one of lifelong boredom and seemed to her as bleak as the cold winds that swept across the fens, even at times as terrible as the great Cathedral in whose shadow she must live and die. For at that time she did not love the Cathedral and in her fantasy life the city had merely been the hub from which her radiant dreams stretched out to the wide wheel of the world. What should she do? Her question was not a cry of despair but a genuine and honest wish to know.

She never knew what put it into her head that she, unloved, should love. Religion for her parents, and therefore for their children, was not much more than a formality and it had not occurred to her to pray about her problem, and yet from somewhere the idea came as though in answer to her question, and sitting in Blanche's bower with the cat she dispassionately

PATTERN OF PEOPLE

considered it. Could mere loving be a life's work? Could it be a career like marriage or nursing the sick or going on the stage? Could it be adventure? Christians were commanded to love, it was something laid upon them that they had to do whether they liked it or not. They had to love, as a wife had to obey her husband and an actress had to speak her lines when the curtain rose, and she was a Christian because she had been baptised and confirmed in the Cathedral and went to matins every Sunday in her best bonnet. But what was love? Was there anything or anybody that she herself truly loved?

A rather shattering honesty was as much a part of her as her strong will and her humour, and the answer to this question was that she loved the cat and Blanche's bower. She fed the cat and nursed him when he was sick, and she dusted the bower and kept a beau-pot of flowers on the window-sill. Her eyes were always on them, watchful for beauty to adore, for the ripple of the muscles under the cat's striped fur, the movement of sun and shadow on the walls of the bower. And watchful for danger too. She had got badly hurt once rescuing the cat from a savage dog, and when the bower's ceiling got patched with damp she gave her father no rest until he sent for the builder to mend the roof. She was concerned for them both and had so identified herself with them that they seemed part of her. Making a start with the cat, was it possible to make of this concern and identification a deliberate activity that should pass out in widening circles, to her parents and the servants and the brothers and sisters and their families, to the city and its people, the Cathedral, even at last perhaps to God Himself? It came to her in a flash that it must be wonderful to hold God and be held by Him, as she held the cat in her arms rubbing her cheek against his soft fur, and was in turn held within the safety and quietness of the bower. Then she was shocked by the irreverence of her thought, and tried to thrust it away. But she did not quite succeed. From that day onwards it remained warm and glowing at the back of her mind.

So she took a vow to love. Millions before her had taken the same simple vow but she was different from the majority because she kept her vow, kept it even after she had discovered the cost of simplicity. Until now she had only read her Bible as a pious

168

exercise, but now she read it as an engineer reads a blueprint and a traveller a map, unemotionally because she was not emotional, but with a profound concentration because her life depended on it. Bit by bit over a period of years, that seemed to her long, she began to get her scaffolding into place. She saw that all her powers, even those which had seemed to mitigate against love, such as her shrewdness which had always been quick to see the faults of others, her ambition and self-will, could by a change of direction be bound over in service to the one overmastering purpose. She saw that she must turn from herself, and began to see something of the discipline that that entailed, and found too as she struggled that no one and nothing by themselves seemed to have the power to entirely hold her when she turned to them.

It was then that the central figure of the gospels, a historical figure whom she deeply revered and sought to imitate, began at rare intervals to flash out at her like live lightning from their pages, frightening her, turning the grave blueprint into a dazzle of reflected fire. Gradually she learned to see that her fear was not of the lightning itself but what it showed her of the nature of love, for it dazzled behind the stark horror of Calvary. At this point, where so many vowed lovers faint and fail, Mary Montague went doggedly on over another period of years that seemed if possible longer and harder than the former period. At some point along the way, she did not know where because the change came so slowly and gradually, she realized that He had got her and got everything. His love held and illumined every human being for whom she was concerned, and whom she served with the profound compassion which was their need and right, held the Cathedral, the city, every flower and leaf and creature, giving it reality and beauty. She could not take her eyes from the incredible glory of His love. As far as it was possible for a human being in this world she had turned from herself. She could say, "I have been turned," and did not know how very few can speak these words with truth.

Through most of her life no one noticed anything unusual about her, though they found her increasingly useful. The use her family made of her, however, was more or less unconscious, because she was always there, like Fountains itself, and because she was as unobtrusive as the old furniture whose quiet beauty seemed painted on the dusk of the ancient house. She was just Mary, plain, dumpy, lame, one of those people who do not seem to alter much as the years pass because they have no beauty to lose. The sons and daughters of the house enjoyed their visits home because Fountains was a peaceful sort of place. The servants were happy and contented and the work of the house ran smoothly. The grandchildren, especially those whose parents were in India and who were sent home to be looked after by their Aunt Mary, were more perceptive than their elders. When in after years they looked back on Fountains as upon a lost paradise they saw the face and figure of Aunt Mary as inseparable from it and they knew that they loved her. A few of them loved her as they loved no one else. Each one of them was quite sure that she loved him as she loved no one else; which was true, for seeing as she did the love of God perfectly in each creature of His creation and care she could love the creature as though it were all that existed, and she loved almost without favouritism.

Almost, because she was human. There was one who was dearer than all the rest, her brother Clive who had pushed her down the tower stairs. He, alone among her brothers and sisters, grew to be more perceptive even than the children, because he never forgot what he had done. He intuitively knew that she endured constant pain and slept badly, though no one else knew; her strong will had enabled her not only never to speak of it but also for all practical purposes to overcome it; and he knew also, because she made him understand this, that she set some sort of value on her pain and thanked him for it. Just what its value was to her he could not understand, because explanation of the inexplicable was never Mary's strong point. It deepened love, she said, and sharpened prayer by making them as piercing as itself if drawn into them. But this was beyond him. What was not beyond him was delighted comprehension of her impish humour, which she was too shy to reveal to many. With him she gave it full play and they had great fun together over the years. He alone of the family did not marry and though they met seldom, because as a soldier he was abroad a great deal, the bond between them grew stronger as they grew older. In late middle-age his health failed and he came home to

Fountains. In his forty-eighth year he died a hard death after a long hard illness through which Mary and her faithful old maid Sarah nursed him, and after his death darkness enveloped Mary.

She was forty-five years old and she had not believed that such a thing could happen to her. Through the years her faith had grown so strong that she had not believed that she could lose it. The living light that had made love possible had seemed too glorious ever to go out, yet now it had gone and left her in darkness and the loneliness of life without love was to her a horror quite indescribable. It had a stifling nightmare quality. A cold darkness, she thought, would have been easier to bear, but this hot thick darkness brought one near to the breaking of the mind. It had been for nothing, she thought. It was not true. It had been for nothing. The wells of water to which she had always turned for refreshment had dried up. When she opened her Bible it was just a book like any other, and that revered historical figure, as self-deceived as herself, was as dead as Clive, killed like him by suffering so great that she could not let herself think of it, for they were not the only ones to pass into nothingness through that meaningless agony. Even the current cat could give her no joy, for it was spring and when she tried to find a little comfort in the garden she was perpetually stumbling over the young birds that he had killed. The Cathedral, huge and glowering, oppressed her with a sense of the colossal idiocy of man and she could have wept to think of all the men who had suffered and died to build it. Why pour out all that blood and treasure for the glory of a God Who if He existed at all existed only as a heartless tyrant? She went on going to the Cathedral services as usual but they bored her so intolerably that she could scarcely sit through them. She went, she supposed, from force of habit. It was part of her routine.

Later she realized how much men and women owe to mere routine. She had for years led an extremely disciplined life, and now discipline held her up as irons hold the body of a paralytic. No one except Sarah and Doctor Jenkins found her at all changed. Her parents, old and ailing now, her father growing blind and her mother bedridden, propped their whole weight upon her just as usual, the old people in the workhouse and in Swithins Lane listened as eagerly as ever for the sound of her pony-carriage

coming down the cobbled lane, and found her just as satisfactory a
source of supply as she had ever been. But Sarah kept trying to
make her put her feet up on the sofa, and Doctor Jenkins called
upon her on his own initiative one day and placed a bottle of pink
medicine on her escritoire.

"What's that for?" she asked a little tartly.

Doctor Jenkins was a young shy man in those days but he was
not abashed by the tartness, unusual though it was, because he
loved Miss Montague. When he had first come to the city as
assistant to old Doctor Wharburton he had felt scared and lonely
and had not liked the place, but as soon as Captain Montague's
gout and Mrs. Montague's asthma had brought him to Fountains
he began to feel different. He had had no idea what an intelligent
and attractive fellow he was until he had met Miss Montague.
Now he sat down in his favourite chair, realized afresh how
likable he was, relaxed happily and told her at length how
exhausted she was by her brother's long illness, and by her father's
gout and blindness and her mother's asthmatic heart and querulous temper. She must rest more and take this tonic. "It has iron
in it," he finished.

"I'll take it, Tom," Miss Montague promised for love of him,
though she did not believe a word of it.

Yet at the end of the first bottle of tonic she began to wonder if
there was something in it. She was used to feeling exhausted and
paid no attention to it, for it was her normal state, but this
abysmal fatigue both of body and mind was not her normal state.
She was in darkness but how much had the miasma of fatigue
contributed to it? Was it possible that a bottle of tonic and putting
one's feet up could affect one's faith in God? Shocked at the
unaccustomed way in which her thoughts were dwelling on herself
she drove down to the workhouse in her pony-carriage with six
flannel petticoats and a dozen packets of tea and baccy. Coming
back up Cockspur Street her eyes were caught by the window of
the new little shop which had just been opened by young Mr.
Isaac Peabody. It was a very long time since her attention had
been caught by anything, but there was a clock there shaped like a
Greek lyre and Clive had taught her to love all things Greek.
Before she knew what she was doing she had stopped the pony-

carriage, climbed out, and was gazing at the clock, fascinated by the circle of bright birds whose bodies would never fall and die. The lark at the summit of the lyre was so beautifully fashioned that she could see the quiver of his spread wings and the pulsing of his throat as the song poured from his open beak. . . .

She opened the shop door and walked in and young Mr. Isaac Peabody came forward from the room behind the counter, an oddly bird-like creature with arms that were too long for him. He moved them up and down as he talked as though they were wings and he meant to take off at any moment. It showed how much good the tonic had done her that the moment she set eyes on him she knew she had a new friend and was glad. A short while ago she had wanted no new friends. Somehow, against her conscience, she bought the Lyre clock, and when she reached Fountains the delighted Sarah carried it up the stairs for her and put it on her escritoire, and she sat down on the sofa and put her feet up and looked at it. From then onwards, whenever she had a few moments, she put her feet up and looked at it and the bright ring of birds seemed to gather all the sunshine to itself.

That was not the end of her darkness, which continued for a long while yet, but it was the first bit of comfort in it. She began to sleep better and sometimes now when she woke in the mornings it was not to that indescribable despair but to a quiet sadness, and with the name of her God upon her lips. But it was autumn before joy was restored to her again, and then it was not the same joy.

She found herself, one wet Wednesday afternoon in October, with an hour to spare, an unusual state of things in her hard-pressed life. She was to have taken the chair at a women's missionary meeting but the speaker had been taken ill and the meeting was cancelled. She had arranged for Sarah to sit with her mother, and for a friend of her father's to have tea with him and read aloud until she came back, and the wild idea came to her that she would do with this hour just what she pleased. But she must go out, for her household did not know that the meeting had been cancelled. Feeling like a truant from school she put on her bonnet and cloak, found her umbrella and let herself out of the old front door into the cool dark cavern of the Porta, the archway that led into the Close. Beyond it was a drizzle of fine rain and Worship

Street looked grey and dismal, but in the greyness of the Close there were gleams of gold, as though sunrays were enmeshed in the rain, because the bright leaves were not yet fallen. So she went that way, limping slowly under her umbrella, and the air seemed fresh and sweet after her mother's overheated bedroom. But where should she go? She could only go a short way, for now that the rheumatism had settled so firmly in her bad leg and her back such a thing as going for a walk was not possible for her. She could call at any of the houses in the Close and be warmly welcomed but she felt too tired for social calls. She thought she would go to the south door of the Cathedral and sit there on the stone bench and talk to the old bedesman, old Bob Hathaway whom she was very fond of, for she found poor people much more restful than the well-to-do. She walked slowly, for there was that whole hour stretching before her with its blessed emptiness, but even so she was tired when she reached the south door and found it oddly comforting to have old Bob clucking at her like a fussy hen, helping her to shake the wet out of her skirts and put her umbrella down. He was a crusty old man, without the courtesy of Tom Hochicorn who years later was to succeed him, but he was almost as fond of her as she was of him and the scolding he gave her was a pleasure.

"Abroad in all this wet!" he growled. "Why don't ee wear pattens, ma'am?"

"They don't suit my rheumatism, Bob," she explained.

"Sitting on this 'ere cold stone at your age, ma'am!" he went on wrathfully.

"You sit on it," she said, "and you're older than I am."

"Old enough to be your father, ma'am," he said, "which is why I'm giving ee a piece o' my mind."

He went on giving it for some while, and then they talked of rheumatism in general and Bob's in particular, and the terrible wind he had after fried onions, and Miss Montague was just beginning most wonderfully to enjoy Bob when she had the misfortune to sneeze and he got angry with her again. Either she must go home, he said, or she must go into the Cathedral and have a bit of a warm by the brazier. It was lit. She did not want to go home and so to please him she said she would go into the

Cathedral for a few moments. He opened the door for her and she went in.

It was very dark in the Cathedral, except for the glow of the large charcoal braziers that were lit here and there in its vastness. They did practically nothing to conquer the cold of the great place but they were pretty as flowers. She made her way to the nearest and held out her chilly hands to its comfort. It burned beside the carved archway that led into the chantry of the duchess Blanche and glowed rosily upon the stone, just as the sunset glowed upon the stone of Blanche's bower at home at Fountains. Miss Montague moved forward into the chantry and sat down on the old rush-seated chair that was just inside. It had a hole in it, for in these days . . . the Cathedral was not well cared for, and her spreading skirts stirred up the dust. Then the dust settled, and with it the silence, and she realized that she had never before been quite alone in the Cathedral. There were the old bedesmen at the doors but they seemed far away, and it was dark. Vast curtains of shadow fell from the invisible roof and they seemed to move like a tide of dark water. She felt very lonely and she wished she had the cat on her lap.

In the dimness she could just see the little figure of the duchess Blanche lying on her tomb, by herself because her husband had been buried beside the High Altar, but not lonely because there was a dog at her feet. Her hands lay on her breast placed palm to palm in prayer. . . . It was too dark to see it now but Miss Montague knew how lovely it was, small and delicate like the little duchess herself, with cherubs in all the nooks and crannies. Cromwell's men had defaced these, and Blanche's praying hands, but they had not succeeded in spoiling the chantry's beauty, only in giving it a look of battered but enduring patience.

"You've been here so long," Miss Montague said to Blanche, "praying with those wounded hands." For though her mind told her that Blanche was either nowhere, or somewhere else, but anyhow not here, yet she could not this afternoon quite get rid of the feeling that Blanche was here. And high up in the darkness that her sight could not penetrate He was there upon the rood. Her hands folded in her lap Miss Montague shut her eyes, for she was very tired. She ceased to feel lonely. Blanche was here, and the Man on the rood, sharing the same darkness with her and with a vast multitude of people whom she seemed to know and love. How much more friendly it is when you cannot see, thought Miss Montague, and how much closer we are to Him. Why should we always want a light? He chose darkness for us, darkness for the womb and of the stable, darkness in the garden, darkness on the cross and in the grave. Why do I demand certainty? That is not faith. Why do I want to understand? How can I understand this great web of sin and ugliness and love and suffering and joy and life and death when I don't understand the little tangle of good and evil that is myself? I've enough to understand. I understand that He gave me light that I might turn to Him, for without light I could not have seen to turn. I have seen creation in His light. He shared His light with me that I, turned, might share with Him the darkness of His redemption. Why did I despair? What do I want? If it is Him I want He is here, not only love in light illuming all that He has made but love in darkness dying for it. . . . And she said, I will learn to pray.

It was a promise. She said, Please may I begin to learn here with Blanche, and she whose prayer until now had been the murmuring of soothing and much loved words in the tired intervals between one thing and another, or the presentation to Almighty God of inventories of the needs of the city as she drove about it in her pony-carriage, abandoned herself for the sake of those she loved to silence and the dark, understanding however dimly that to draw some tiny fraction of the sin of the world into her own being with this darkness was to do away with it.

Bob's hand fell upon her shoulder and she looked up. It was now almost entirely dark in the Cathedral and she saw his anxious puckered face only dimly by the light of the brazier. "Ma'am, ye've been here near an hour," he said crossly.

It had seemed five minutes. She got up with his help and they went back to the south door. He opened her umbrella for her, while she settled her cloak and shook the dust out of her skirts. Then she smiled at him and thanked him and went away into the rain.

[Adapted from *The Dean's Watch* (1960)]

Giovanni

No one but the holy man up on the hill could do anything with Giovanni. He was wild as a leveret and mischievous as a jackdaw, but because he was an attractive small boy quite a number of the kindly people in the Vale of Rietti would have been glad to give him a more permanent home than the temporary shelter he would occasionally accept, if the weather was bad or his stomach empty. Besides, it gave the valley a bad name to have an orphan boy running around apparently uncared for and unloved. But Giovanni did not wish to be cared for, and as for love, he had the birds and animals and the holy man whom men called Brother Francis, and these two loves satisfied his heart. He loved the creatures because they were wild as himself and he loved Brother Francis because he shared his tastes, disliking a roof over his head except in winter, and only then because the fire on the hearth was bright and gay to look at, and loving the sun and moon and stars as though they were his friends. He also liked to sing, and so did Giovanni. Brother Francis would pick up two sticks and pretend they were a viol and a bow, and he would pass the bow across the imaginary strings and he and Giovanni would sing together to the accompaniment that both of them heard very clearly. Brother Francis was always gay with Giovanni and the little boy was sorry that he did not live always in the hermitage on the slope of Monte Rainerio, but only came occasionally to rest and pray. Giovanni always knew when he was there. He knew it as the birds know when food has been put out for them. That is, he knew.

He knew it now. Indeed he had known it in the middle of last night, when he had felt the rain coming through the straw roof of the deserted shepherd's hut where he had curled up to sleep, and his heart had jumped for joy because his friend was here. But he was sorry about the weather because rain seemed all wrong when

177

Brother Francis was there. He loved light, and loved it so much that when Giovanni had asked him once what God was like he had said He was like light. He had said that the glorious sun in the sky is like God the Father, and the sunshine coming down from the sun and warming us through and through is like Christ our Saviour, and that both of Them dwell within the hearts of all men as a gift of light that is God the Holy Spirit. Giovanni had taken this quite literally and when his heart jumped for joy he would see with his inside eyes the leap of a bright flame. And when it had jumped it would die down again and he would see a round, glowing ball lying still like a coal in the fire. This ball would glow with love, or anger or pity, but it only jumped when Giovanni was suddenly happy. But his outside eyes could not see it, and this grieved him, so that at present he preferred the sun and the light of the sun, and he was sorry it was raining.

At the first gleam of a grey dawn he was up and away and scrambling up through the wet woods towards the hermitage. He knew every twist and turn of the rough path and soon saw up above him the caves in the rock that formed the hermitage, and the small stone chapel that Brother Francis had built with his own hands and dedicated to Santa Maria Maddalena. He moved with caution now for Brother Francis did not always come alone to Monte Rainerio; sometimes he brought one or two of the brothers with him, and though they were fond of Giovanni, and had told him with laughter that he was one of them because he ran barefoot about the world, they did sometimes shoo away visitors if Brother Francis was at prayer. Giovanni did not tell on them, though he knew Brother Francis did not like people to be shooed away, because one does not tell on one's brothers, however objectionable they may be.

But the coast seemed clear and he came quietly to the chapel, where Brother Francis was usually to be found in the early mornings. He was there now. Standing in the doorway Giovanni could see him kneeling before the rough stone altar with his face buried in his hands, and he was weeping. Never having seen his friend anything but merry Giovanni was shocked and scared, and with that live coal inside his heart burning with pity he forgot about not interrupting Brother Francis at his prayers and ran to him, kneeling down beside him and tugging at the cord that bound his brown habit about his waist. "What's the matter, Brother Francis?" he demanded. "Have you toothache?"

Brother Francis looked down at the child kneeling beside him. "My son," he said, "I should have preferred toothache to this grief."

"What grief?" demanded Giovanni.

It was typical of Francis of Assisi that he should answer the child's question with the truth. Child-like at heart he did not distinguish very clearly between boys and grown men. They were all his children.

"There are many of my sons who are tired of going barefoot about the world," he said. "They wish me to change the rules of our Order, that they may have less hardship. They are weary of following the example of Our Lord Jesus Christ. I cannot see my way. The light has gone out within me."

A shadow fell upon them. Giovanni looked up and saw that one of the brothers had come in, a man he did not know. He was shivering and oppressed with gloom and raindrops were dripping off the point of his thin nose. He was also extremely angry at finding a wet grubby boy interrupting Brother Francis at his prayers, and he would have boxed the boy's ears had not Giovanni dived under his arm and run away down into the wood, despite Brother Francis's cry to him that he should come back. He wasn't going to come back to have his ears boxed, for he had his dignity to consider. But he bore no ill will against the shivering brother. He must be a new one for the old ones whom he knew, Leo and Juniper and the others, had learnt to control their shivers long ago. It must be the new ones who were tired of following the example of Our Lord Jesus Christ, and in weather like this one could understand how they felt.

All that wet day Giovanni was wondering what he could do to comfort Brother Francis because the light in his heart had gone out. But when he went to sleep that night he hadn't thought of anything, and when he woke up in the morning he still hadn't thought. But the rain had passed in the night and the sun was shining so he forgot his sorrow, leaped up in joy and ran out of the hut.

The sun had not risen very far. It shone in glory just above the trees at the end of the meadow and the whole world was brimming with its light. Giovanni danced up and down in the light and the light warmed him. And then he saw the most wonderful thing. The whole meadow, stretching from his feet to the sun, was sparkling as though it were on fire, as though every wet flower and blade of grass was carrying a tongue of flame. The light was so brilliant that it dazzled the eyes. Blinking, Giovanni bent down and picked a small blue flower with rayed petals that grew at his feet. He looked at it and saw that it held in its heart a globe of light shining and sparkling like the sun. It *was* the sun. And the light of the sun. And so, thought Giovanni, all the flowers and the grasses must have the light of the Holy Spirit inside them just like I have. Perhaps everything has. And then he thought, I'll take it to Brother Francis to comfort him.

He wrapped the flower carefully in a green leaf, keeping it upright so that the light of the Holy Spirit should not fall out, and he ran towards the woods. He climbed up through the trees and today they were sun-shot and beautiful, and smelt warm and fragrant, and all the birds in the world were singing in them. He came in sight of the chapel and saw Brother Francis sitting on the stone doorstep. He was not weeping this morning but his eyes were sad and he did not seem to see Giovanni until the little boy sat down beside him.

"Look, Brother Francis, look!"

Brother Francis sighed and became aware of the excited child beside him. "What have you in the leaf, my son?" he asked, and he tried very hard to sound as curious as Giovanni wanted him to be.

"He's inside what's inside the leaf," whispered Giovanni hoarsely, and he unfolded the leaf and opened the blue petals of the flower. But there was nothing inside now. The raindrop that had looked like the sun had vanished.

"He's gone," said Giovanni, and he let the flower slip through his nerveless fingers to the ground. He was too unhappy to cry but a few unshed tears gathered on his lashes.

Brother Francis stooped and picked up the flower, for he could not endure that it should be trampled on, and he waited. While he waited he looked at the flower and he thought he had never seen anything more beautiful. Within the outer glory of the rayed blue petals the stamens were shaped like a crown of thorns and at the heart, as he held it towards the sun, he saw a pin-prick of light and knew that at dawn it had held a sun-shot raindrop there.

Giovanni swallowed and was able to put the tragedy into words. "God the Holy Spirit has gone out," he said. "I was bringing Him to you and He's gone out."

"He never goes out," said Brother Francis.

"He went out in your heart," retorted Giovanni. "You said so."

Brother Francis looked at Giovanni and he thought how lustrous are the tears of children, lustrous as their love. He stretched out his little finger and with infinite care touched first Giovanni's eyelashes and then the heart of the flower.

"I was mistaken," said Brother Francis. "And you were mistaken when you thought you had not brought Him to me in the heart of this flower. Look!"

Giovanni looked, and at the centre of the flower that Brother Francis was holding up towards the sun was the flame once more, sparkling and brilliant as ever. It was the sun, and the light of the sun.

"I don't understand," said Giovanni.

"Nor do I," said Brother Francis, and then he suddenly began to laugh, and Giovanni began to laugh. They laughed and laughed, and then Brother Francis picked up two sticks, and tucked one under his chin and began to draw the other across it like a bow across a viol. They both heard the music of the viol, and they sang to it. They sang more and more joyously, and so did the birds. The singing ran through the woods, and it was Whitsunday.

[Taken from *The Lost Angel* (1971)]

Cheese and Black Coffee

MICHAEL ROUNDED THE hill and saw the manor-house in front of him at the bottom of a sloping field. He climbed upon the gate of the field and sat and stared. It was a timber-framed house, small for a manor-house but quite perfect, built in the shape of an E, with tall chimneys, and facing south across the river. The steep roof, irregular and stained with red-gold lichen, had dormer windows in it. The big porch which formed the central part of the E, and most of the front of the house, appeared to be covered with wistaria. Behind the house cob walls protected by pent-houses of thatch enclosed the kitchen garden and orchard, and in front of the house yews surrounded a garden that seemed to slope in terraces towards the river. From where he sat Michael could not see the garden behind the yew hedges, or see how its formal loveliness lost itself in the azaleas and rhododendrons down below, nor how upon the east side the garden looked down upon the church tower, and the churchyard with its drift of daffodils. He could only guess at these things from where he sat, and he jumped off the gate and strode across the field. A lark was singing over his head.

As he came nearer, Michael became increasingly aware of dilapidation. His conjecture that the roses had not been pruned for a hundred years was going to prove correct. The yew hedges had not been cut for a long time either. . . .

Yet still there was the scent of flowers, for as he moved forward he found clumps of small purple violets running riot over the edges of the weed-filled flower-beds and the moss grown paths, and there were drifts and pools of daffodils and narcissus in the wild rough grass. The sweetbriar hedges and the standard roses had flung out wild sprays of branches in all directions, but they were glowing with new leaves. The plants in the border were not quite buried. . . .

Somewhere behind him upon one of the flagged paths he heard the pattering of feet, a strange pattering that sounded like a very old lady walking in pattens. There was a swishing sound too, as though long silken skirts fell from step to step. Michael, his back turned, stood still. She was coming. His heart was beating as ridiculously hard as though he were a lover waiting for his sovereign, his lovely goddess. And he knew most certainly that the coming of this old lady did matter to him as much as all that, perhaps more, for by letting him stay or sending him away she had it in her power to save or damn him. So he believed, and though his power of self-dramatisation had led him into disaster time and again, it had at other times given him a sure instinct for the moment when he should play the hero for his own advancement. He stood for a moment, visualising her, the swishing silk dress the same deep ruby as her jewels, her small hand holding it up in front above the pattens, the dark waves of it caressing the stones behind, her peacocks one on each side.

He turned slowly, gracefully, dramatically, ready to bow, and found himself confronting a large white pig. The shock was so great that he bowed to the pig. "Michael Stone, you are the most unutterable ass," he said to himself and bowed again, this time with exaggeration. Then he bowed the third time with real admiration, for it was the most remarkable pig. To his town-bred ignorance a pig was a dirty repulsive brute, and this rosy porcine beauty was a revelation to him of what a pig can be.

"Don't let Josephine go down those steps," called a husky voice.

Recovering from his shock, he was aware that the swishing sound continued, and taking his fascinated eyes from the pig, he looked up and saw the most peculiar old woman swishing away at the nettles behind a rosemary tree with a stick. "The slope is steep down to the river," she continued. "Remember the Gadarene swine?"

"I often do," Michael called back. "I'm full of devils. Have you a large herd?"

"No," said the old woman. "A small one. But they are not to receive your devils, young man. Far too valuable. I show them.

That is why I am exercising Josephine. Keep your devils to yourself, if you please. These nettles have got a real hold here. Who are you, by the way? Have you a message?"

"Yes," said Michael desperately. "I'd come and deliver it, only Josephine seems anxious to go down these steps."

"Stay where you are," commanded the old woman. "Keep your eye on her and I'll come. Though really you could shout it. There's nobody here but the sundial, and it keeps its secrets."

She climbed over a low wall with ease, though Michael perceived her to be of a great age. She stamped her feet on the stones of the terrace, to get the earth off them, and came towards him. She wore a peat-brown tweed coat and skirt, pulled out of shape and faded by work and weather, with the skirt reaching only just below her knees, thick brown worsted stockings and a pair of clumping lace-up boots of the type which Michael up to now had seen only in pictures. A battered felt hat was placed well forward over her forehead and skewered into position above the knot of grey hair at the back of her head with a large hat-pin that protruded several inches each way. The figure and the headgear, though not the face, reminded him instantly of Tenniel's Red Queen. Her small claw-like hands were grimed with dirt. Yet she herself was delightfully fresh and trim, and as she came close to him he could see she wore a blouse of priceless lace, freshly laundered, and that her thick grey hair was carefully brushed and coiled. Her figure was tiny and her little face deeply wrinkled and gipsy-brown, her black eyes keen and sparkling under beautiful arched brows, the sucked-in puckered mouth above the nut-cracker chin matching it in iron determination. Michael knew that once she had had great beauty; vital and compelling and very sure of itself. Even now the vitality and assurance compelled him. He had meant to practise his charms upon this old lady, but instead he found himself being hooked and landed by her own.

"Well now, young man, what is it?" she asked, but though the husky voice was sharp, she seemed in no hurry. She did not belong to a generation that had ever hurried. Her tasks might be herculean, but she had all the time there was for whoever came. She took a gold cigarette-case from her pocket, offered him one and took one herself. As he lit hers and then his own, she watched him not narrowly but with a benevolence that was at the same time both keen and gracious. . . .

"Sit down," she said, motioning with her cigarette towards the steps. "If we sit on them Josephine can't go down them. Also I have reached the age when I'd sooner sit than stand. And you yourself, if I may say so, have been so long standing around in my garden that I wonder you have not sat down before. But you're young. Now where's that pig?"

"She's gone into the gazebo," said Michael.

"She can stay there," said the old lady. "She's had her exercise."

"Do you exercise all the pigs?" asked Michael weakly.

"At present," she said. "Bob Hewitt, my man, is sick, and the boy who comes up from the village is not much good. Do you like pigs?"

"My acquaintance with them has never been intimate," said Michael.

"Nothing but pork and a receptacle for devils, you think. There you are wrong. A pig, young man, when properly treated and rightly understood, is one of the most intelligent and lovable of God's creatures."

She was leaning back against one of the urns beside the steps, regarding him shrewdly and kindly, but he could see how tired she looked.

"I won't keep you," he said humbly and gently. "I have no message. I was simply trespassing." . . .

"And why were you trespassing?"

"I was going to ask you to take me on as your gardener," said Michael baldly, stating a fact and exerting no charm.

"Do you know anything about gardening?"

"Very little."

"Then why should I want you for my gardener?"

"I was not thinking about it from your point of view," said Michael.

"And how were you thinking about it from your own?" she asked. "Did you by any chance think this would be a good place to get rid of those devils you spoke of?"

"That's exactly what I did think," said Michael.

"My dear boy, devils are not so easy to get rid of as you seem to imagine."

"I realize that," said Michael.

"How long have you been in Belmaray?" she asked.

"Since this morning."

"Have you met my great-nephew, the vicar?"

"Yes."

"Did he suggest that I might take you on as my gardener?"

"No," said Michael. "The suggestion was mine. He thought I was joking. And so I was then. But now—well, I'm not joking." He paused and forced himself on. "Though I don't know much about gardening I could learn," he finished desperately.

"You might, of course, be good with the pigs," she said, considering him. "Are you staying anywhere?"

"I had high tea at the Wheatsheaf."

"You left your luggage there?"

"I haven't any luggage except what's in my pocket—just a tooth-brush and so on that I bought yesterday in Silverbridge. I spent last night in Silverbridge."

"And where did you spend the night before that?"

"In prison. I caught the afternoon train from Paddington and left everything I possessed in London."

"Did you possess much?"

"No, not much. A flat and so on. And something in my bank balance. It accumulates while you're in prison."

"So I've heard. But how very odd to leave London without any tooth-brush."

"Leaving was a very sudden decision."

"So I should imagine. How much of this have you told my great-nephew?"

"None of it. He found me hungry on Pizzle bridge, fetched me breakfast from the farm, and then we walked down the road and talked about your rhododendrons. I like rhododendrons and I said in joke that I'd like to be your gardener. I know, of course, that you are Miss Wentworth."

"You can't know much about rhododendrons. When you've planted a rhododendron in the right soil you've planted it in the right soil, and that's all there is to it. With pigs, now, it's different.

The proper care of a pedigree pig is a life's work for an intelligent man. Where's Josephine?"

"Still in the gazebo."

"What's your name?"

"Michael Stone," said Michael, gazing down the field with a face as still and hard as his own name.

"Never heard of you," said Miss Wentworth. "And I would be obliged if you would take another cigarette and stop gazing into the middle distance like that tiresome young man Orestes."

"It was not murder I was in for," Michael assured her. "Though I was in for a very serious offence."

"There are worse things than murder," said Miss Wentworth placidly. . . . She looked at him shrewdly. "You'd be better asleep," she said. "A good deal to make up, by the looks of you. And that's a nasty cough you have. But I've a good deal to do before I can get your sheets aired. My pig man is sick, as I told you, and Jane Prescott only comes in the mornings."

She got up more nimbly than he did, and his mingled shame and reluctance made him stumble awkwardly as he came up the steps and held out his hand. "Good-bye, Miss Wentworth," he said. "I won't say I didn't mean it, because I did. I did come here meaning to impose myself on you in some capacity or other. I thought I'd try it on. I don't know what I expected to happen. Not what has happened. I didn't know I had enough decency left in me to feel so profoundly ashamed."

"Shame is a good thing," said the old lady, taking his hand. "When it's your own, that is. To shame another is one of the worst of crimes."

He had a good hand, well shaped, broad and long, while hers was frail, light and dry as an autumn leaf, yet his shook so much in hers that she tightened her grip. "Even that can be forgiven," she said. "Shame can be offered for shame. No, I am not saying good-bye. I am holding you where you are. I shall find an able-bodied young man exceedingly useful, however ignorant." Feeling his hand once more steady, she dropped it abruptly. "Josephine!"

Obedient as a dog, Josephine appeared from the gazebo and trotted towards them, and Miss Wentworth handed Michael the stick. "Now take her up to the house. Don't strike her. Touch her gently on the right flank if you want her to go to the left, and the other way on. Let me see if you have the makings of a pig-man in you. . . . Through the front door and out of the garden door. . . ."

"Through the front door," whispered Michael. "Amen."

Josephine went sedately along the flagged paths, obedient to every light touch of the stick. Coming after her, observing her noble proportions from behind, Michael perceived that she was indeed a magnificent animal with a skin like pale pink satin. "I expect I wash her," he thought. . . .

Following at the tail of the procession, where he could not see her, Miss Wentworth said gruffly, "I should apologise too. I was brought up never to mention money in conversation, never to mention health and never to ask questions. I asked at least twenty. I ask your pardon, and I will never put another question to you except this final one—do you like your coffee black or white?"

"Black," said Michael.

"Good," said Miss Wentworth. "I never trust a man who takes his coffee white."

Michael, who had known many trustworthy men who did, had no wish to argue the point. It was enough for him to know that she trusted him. . . .

The front door of grey weathered oak was closed. . . . Miss Wentworth turned the handle and preceded by Josephine they went into the old porch, as large as a room with its recessed windows with seats in them. The inner door was open and a wide flagged passage led through the depth of the house to the open door into the kitchen garden. Josephine trotted purposefully down and Michael followed after.

"Come back when you have shut her in her sty in the orchard," Miss Wentworth called after him. "You will probably find me upstairs in the linen-closet." . . .

Having dealt with Josephine, Michael went back the way he had come, through the stable yard into the orchard and from there into the vegetable garden. Under one of the mulberry bushes he stood still. It was intensely quiet, and, with the sky so overcast, twilight seemed not far away. It was growing cold with already a hint of coming rain, and the scent of violets came to him from somewhere. . . .

188

A window in the house opened and a gruff voice called, "Is there a broccoli down there?"

"A gross of them," Michael called back.

"Bring me one. Do you like them with cheese?"

Michael, stooping to cut one with his pocket knife, called back, "If that's a thing trustworthy men like, yes."

In a few strides he was under the window and looking up at her. She had taken off her hideous hat and in the dim light her face had almost a look of youth. . . . For a moment he wished with all his heart that she was young. Then he did not. Where would her deftness have been then, her wisdom and compassion? . . . These things come to their full glory only when the pride of life is past.

She smiled at him. "I did not need that reassurance," she said.

[Adapted from *The Rosemary Tree* (1956)]

Copyright Sources

Woven from the Past

'Lucy in London' is adapted from *The Child from the Sea*, © 1970 by Elizabeth Goudge.

'The Three Grey Men' is taken from *At the Sign of the Dolphin*, first published 1947. All rights reserved.

'The Children and the Painter' is adapted from *The White Witch*, © 1958 by Elizabeth Goudge.

'The Hub of the Wheel' is adapted from *Gentian Hill*, copyright 1950 by Elizabeth Goudge.

A Chain of Children

'Picnic with Albert' and 'The New Moon' are both taken from *Make-Believe*, first published 1949. All rights reserved.

'Island Holiday' is adapted from *The Joy of the Snow*, © 1974 by Elizabeth Goudge.

'Lost—One Angel' is taken from *The Lost Angel*, © 1971 by Elizabeth Goudge.

'Looking at the Little Things' is adapted from *The Scent of Water*, © 1963 by Elizabeth Goudge.

Designs of the Heart

'Escape for Jane' is taken from *White Wings*, first published 1952. All rights reserved.

'An Artist in Love' is adapted from *The Heart of the Family*, copyright 1953 by Elizabeth Goudge.

'A Pedlar's Pack' is taken from *White Wings*, first published 1952. All rights reserved.

Patchwork of Portraits

'The Man Who Loved Clocks' and 'Miss Montague' are both adapted from *The Dean's Watch*, © 1960 by Elizabeth Goudge.

'Giovanni' is taken from *The Lost Angel*, © 1971 by Elizabeth Goudge.

'Cheese and Black Coffee' is adapted from *The Rosemary Tree*, copyright 1956 by Elizabeth Goudge.